Last Flight Out

Last Flight Out

A NOVEL

ROBERT ERINGER

Bartleby Press
Washington • Baltimore

Cover design by Ross Feldner

ISBN 978-0935437-56-0
Library of Congress Control Number: 2019937028

Published by:
Bartleby Press
PO Box 858
Savage, Maryland 20763
800-953-9929
www.BartlebythePublisher.com

Printed in the United States of America

In Memory
of those who perished during the Montecito Mudslide
9 January 2018

PART ONE

1.

Let's begin with me sitting inside a windowless hearing room that is awash with harsh fluorescent light, the kind that steals your energy and irritates your eyes, and a round white clock—there's always one of those—telling the time in slow motion. This abomination is made all the worse by the presence of a Hearing Officer that possesses the power to slice and dice—with me as the system's intended victim—boxed in by stark white walls that characterize the whitewash underway.

Everything, in my mind anyway, is black and white and varying shades of gray, mostly dark not light.

This is a shake-down-in-progress, the ex-manager of my bar and his sleazy contingency lawyer trying to make a case for fifty-grand over policies *he* insisted on implementing after I hired him, that is, waiving my standard waivers pertaining to employee meal and rest breaks—common in the bar biz—and then complaining about the absence of meal and rest breaks after I fired his butt for slamming shots—three in a row—while on duty behind the bar, a violation of Alcoholic Beverage Control, another state agency always looking to persecute the very bar owners that underwrite its existence. Dare I add the ex-manager was also having affairs with two female bartenders, both of whom he'd made pregnant? And he wasn't stopping there, but striving to recruit a full-on harem, using my bar as the setting for his personal playground and spawning center.

Yet *I'm* the one in the hot seat.

But let's take it back a bit further.

I always thought it would be fun to own a bar of my own: a real old-fashioned iconic neighborhood saloon, no food, just booze, well maybe a jar of pickled eggs, if only for ambience.

But I soon learned that running any kind of small business in the State of California is about walking blind-folded through a minefield of trivial rules and regulations that detonate like landmines no matter how hard you try, at great expense, to walk a straight path.

Corporations have in-house lawyers to deflect govern-ment bureaucracy, and bureaucrats at every level know it, and that's why they fixate on the little guy, mom-and-pops, easy pickings and high volume success stats for meeting quotas and earning bonuses—almost as if there's a conspiracy between government and big chains to corporatize just about everything involving money into a plastic and disposable-oriented society where everyone descends into perpetual debt, shopping at Walmart and Costco and eating sugar and shit at Jack in the Box, Little Caesar's and KFC.

What should be an hour's worth of testimony turns into a whole day of petty banter under the arched, disapproving eyebrows of a sixty-something post-menopausal babushka who, presiding from on high, ominously scribbles notes when not drilling her eyes into mine as if I'm either still in school, belong back in school, or that I got hauled into her courtroom after going on a shooting rampage inside a school.

During an afternoon recess, I walk outside for fresh air and power my phone to check messages, one of which is from my bookkeeper, which I return.

"It's going okay," I tell him, assuming he called for an update on the ludicrous Labor Hearing, about which he'd warned, *In California they always side with the ex-employee no matter what the facts.* "I think the Hearing Officer sees through all their nonsense."

"Good, but that's not why I'm calling," says my bookkeeper. "The State Board of Equalization wants to audit you."

"Who are *they?*"

"The sales tax people."

"Why?"

"Business is down since you bought the place."

He means since the fool I fired destroyed our customer base with his poor white trash machismo.

"It probably got red flagged because they think the owner—you—is skimming cash," he continues. "But don't worry, we've been doing everything by the book from the start and our accounts are squeaky clean. Oh, and can you pop another four-grand into the business account? We have that refrigeration bill to pay."

When I first bought the bar, half its customers were drug-dealers, drunks and gang-bangers with Marilyn Monroe as their tattoo of choice because the legendary Hollywood bombshell's initials, in their demented minds, stand for *Mexican Mafia*.

Some of them got into fistfights every weekend, not because they're mad at one another but because they *like* to fight, to inflict and feel pain as a means of getting their endorphins flowing. I got rid of them to make way for a better class of people, the hipster crowd, with karaoke and live music, new carpet and fine art, cleaned it up really good. All I got in return was the discovery that people who go to bars like mine don't want art or *cleaned up really good.* They come for one thing only: Stiff cheap drinks and a chaser, and maybe a football game in the kind of down-and-dingy environment that makes them feel at home.

Anyway, I'm getting bogged down with too much context, so back to my bookkeeper telling me we're about to get audited by a state that desperately needs to extort money because they're not getting enough for their bloated programs from legitimate taxation.

"I can handle it," he says. "But I need all your records, can you bring them over?"

And I'm thinking, what kind of masochist buys a bar in the State of California—or *anywhere* for that matter in a country that, as Kurt Vonnegut once put it, "is being managed to death." And I'm thinking maybe I should just close it down; see how they feel about *no* sales tax.

So, I go back into the hearing room—my own personal Auschwitz—and listen to my ex-manager whine and snort like a warthog about me supposedly telling him not to list all his hours on the time card and to order our bartenders to do the same—a blatant lie most likely fabricated on the spot because his meal-and-rest-break blather isn't holding water and his case is disintegrating around him. Fortunately, I'd hired a legal eagle (think four-grand to defend myself from baseless charges, the American way) and my guy has done his homework, unlike the ex-manager's lazy, septuagenarian ambulance-chaser (suffering pre-Alzheimer's from the sound of him), who hasn't bothered to study the documented evidence—like time-cards—that conflicts with his client's own testimony.

By the time it's over, around four o'clock, my whole day is shot. I unknot my tie, a useless blood-constricting garment I'd otherwise have no use for on the American Riviera, and say goodbye to my lawyer, who seems satisfied even though there won't be a ruling "for probably five or six months," he tells me—because the Labor Commission is clogged up with thousands of other petty complaints and hearings like mine, our taxes squandered by proliferating bureaucrats with state-paid health care programs, high-end pensions, and every other Friday off.

I again switch on my phone and listen to a stream of voice messages while driving home. Mostly, they're from my wife and daughter, alternating like dueling banjos, without harmony, an old tune with a new flourish, each attempting to lure me into their disharmony, as if my main role in life is supposed to be their histrionics conductor.

Arriving home is like getting conscripted into a battle zone and, having ventured through no man's land before, I know they won't be satisfied until they goad me into cacophony. And since my nerves are already frazzled from too much fluorescent light, not enough fresh air, and bald-faced prevarication, it doesn't take too long before you have three people hollering instead of two, oh the futility.

I'm already defeated, even before walking in, so I raise my hands in surrender, turn around, and head back out the door

"You're crazy!" my wife shouts, her parting volley.

And I wish I were, because if so I could be taken away from here and checked into somewhere quiet for a few days, perhaps a full week, maybe the rest of my life...

2.

climb back into my Jeep, which is now, like me this day, starting to fall apart (just days after the warranty ran out), and I aim myself toward one of my regular watering holes. If I'm going to drink booze it is best to stay close to home in a town where DUI enforcement is downright draconian due to the state's penchant for revenue collection because, if necessary, I can leave my car behind, walking distance.

The Honor Bar is a good fit because it stocks Monkey47 gin, my libation of choice this energy-suck of a day, plus Scottie is on duty in a penguin suit and poised to mix me a martini without my usual song-and-dance about how I like it served: up, a twist, don't shake it, maybe a stir, leave the shaker with strainer on the bar, I'll pour it myself—and you still get a tip.

My gaze turns from the last golden rays of a sun preparing to set through wooden blinds to their vintage Stars and Stripes, the original thirteen colonies, framed beneath glass on the wall nearby, and I think of President John F. Kennedy, whose assassination—to my mind—was the pivotal point in America's steady decline into big government-Wall Street rip-offs, decay and official-dumb.

A television set across the bar flickers, an old black-and-white movie, something I may have seen once called *Pandora's Box* amid an aroma of ginger and sesame from Thai noodles served to a patron nearby.

Harris strolls in after I've taken a couple of sips and nails a stool next to mine and immediately starts gabbing in that intense way of his full of nervous energy, a pock-marked face reminding me of a moon blasted by hundreds of asteroids. He has a thing for one of the young female bartenders so, mercifully, he fixates more on her than on me, fumbling to perpetuate a one-sided dialogue oblivious to the fact that she—forty years his junior—is already spooked by previous encounters with him.

Conveniently (for herself, not me), she gets busy tending to other barflies, so Harris reverts to me even though I'm trying to avoid his gaze by looking elsewhere.

"Where's Andrew this evening?" Harris asks me.

I shrug. "Who knows?"

"But he's your bodyguard, isn't he?"

"No," I say.

"Yes, he is."

"No, he's not."

"Then why is he always here with you?"

"Andrew's tough to shake."

"Because he's your bodyguard."

"I don't need a bodyguard."

"Then why do you have one?" says Harris.

"I don't."

"Yes, you do," Harris insists. "That's why Andrew always wears one glove."

"Is it?"

"Why else would he wear only one glove?"

"I don't know. You'd have to ask Andrew."

"You must know," says Harris, "because he's your bodyguard."

"No, he's not my bodyguard."

"So, what's with the glove?"

This is now comical—to me, at least.

"Who cares if Andrew wears a glove," I say, "or even if he's my bodyguard, which he isn't." I chuckle. "Maybe the glove is for gripping his steering wheel? Or maybe he uses it to jerk off? Truth is, I don't give a crap what his glove is for, why should you?"

"Because he's your bodyguard."

I give up, because Harris is now *beyond* comical. "If you say so." I try to wave him away so that I may contemplate my martini.

"You're not being above board with me," Harris growls.

"Huh?" I study his equine-like face, trying to find something, anything that may conceivably explain his absurdly aggressive stance. But I discern only disturbance. "What's going on with you?" I ask.

"You're not being above board with me," he says, louder than before.

And then, of all people, Andrew sweeps in, surfer dude without a board, fresh from a doobie, takes the other stool next to mine.

Harris leans his taut torso over the bar around me toward the unsuspecting stoner. "So, where's your glove Andrew? Let's see your glove."

Andrew raises his hands, as bewildered as me, no glove. "What are you talking about?"

"Ah, you're not wearing it now." Harris looks down, momentarily defeated, and up again. "But you're his bodyguard, aren't you," he taunts. "Admit it."

Andrew, less patient than I with people who obviously cannot find a few of their marbles, isn't having any of this blather. In fact, the one night I hired Andrew as a doorman at my bar he disappeared the moment he saw a fight brewing. Not exactly bodyguard material. "I don't know what the hell you're talking about, Harris."

"Your glove, Andrew."

"Even if I was wearing a glove, Harris, what the hell does it have to do with you?"

"I already suggested that to him," I say, attempting levity while trying to alert Scottie with my eyes that something is amiss and escalation possible. But Scottie is already on it, as bartenders are trained to be, an ear cocked toward the bizarre banter going on among our triad.

Harris abruptly de-stools to confront Melanie, the assistant manager, insisting that she accompany him outside for a palaver.

Soon after, Harris is gone, and Melanie is whispering to Scott.

A few minutes later, when Scottie leans in to enquire about whether I'd like another drink, I say, "What was *that* about?"

Scottie shakes his head. "Very strange," he whispers. "He told Melanie I'm part of plot to kill him."

"*You?*"

Scottie nods. "Me and the female bartender he seems to like."

"Why you. And her?"

"He told Melanie we'd *have* to know about the plot

to kill him to allow it to happen, which makes us a part of it."

"Dare I ask—do I fit in somehow?"

Scottie nods. "Yes, you do," he continues to whisper. "Harris told Melanie *you* are the person behind the plot to kill him."

"He said *what?*"

"And he said Andrew's involved, too." Scottie reflects on this for a few moments, mildly puzzled. "I don't think Harris was drunk when he came in here—and I served him only one drink."

I shake my head. "This isn't about alcohol," I say. "You don't get Harris's mindset by drinking too much."

"No?"

"No. You get it from psychiatric meds. Strike that. You get it from going *off* psychiatric meds." The gravity of this sinks in. "Harris really thinks I'm plotting to kill him?"

Scottie nods. "And I'm supposedly part of it."

"Well, I sure hope he's not planning a preemptive strike. Are you going to take any precautions, like maybe not serving him anymore?"

Scottie shrugs. "Melanie wants to play it by ear."

Her ear hasn't heard enough?

I'm thinking, in my bar, if a customer believed my bartenders and other regular patrons were part of a plot to kill him and he was clearly off his meds, he'd be eighty-sixed, effective immediately, don't come back, ever. Booze and crazy are never a good mix.

This is a reminder—if we need a reminder—that mental illness is all around us, whether it is collective (think government bureaucracy) or individual (Harris)—or as Mark Twain, an old favorite of mine, once put it, "We're all mad. When we remember that, the mysteries of life disappear and life stands explained."

I drain my martini, leave Scottie a five-buck tip, and stroll to my car, my peripheral version attuned to a potential "preemptive" ambush—think Harris with a chainsaw—what a day.

I intend to take a right turn in the direction of my home but on impulse swing left, cruise the main drag thinking maybe I'll loop the long way home, but when I reach the circle I change my mind and ramp onto Interstate 101 toward Santa Barbara.

Traffic is light. Maybe I'll get off near State Street, drop in somewhere for a glass of wine, take my chances with the bacon. But as I roll past the downtown exits, I skip them, one-by-one, thinking maybe I'll pop into my own bar. Nearing that particular exit, I recognize that, in my frame of mind, I'd probably just get aggravated by something, like the bartenders over-pouring for bigger tips—and I'm already aggravated enough—so I race onward, feeling unbound for the first time since awakening this morning from a sweet dream.

My phone is chiming over and over again—*Home*—but instead of answering I finally click the sound off.

Just keep going. This voice in my head reinforces the resolve of my right foot, firmly planted on the gas pedal, pushing eighty.

A green road sign sporting a white airplane uplifts my mood, an inspiration of sorts, and I roll with it, literally, ramping off at the airport exit onto Route 217, which takes me to a park on a cliff overlooking the ocean. I pull into a parking space and switch off the engine and just sit quietly with the window down, inhaling salt sea air, starting to feel sleepy beneath a sky full of twinkling stars; a vision that momentarily reminds me of the opening sequence of *The Twilight Zone*, my favorite television series from when I was a kid.

And I'm thinking, *at what point exactly did the world—mine in particular—go completely nuts?*

3.

A small jet on its final approach into Santa Barbara Municipal Airport passes just fifty yards over my car and the sheer energy of its engines vibrates my bones, invigorating me into an altered frame of mind, maybe a new direction elsewhere.

I restart my Jeep, ease onto Sandspit Road and spin left toward the airport's long-term parking lot with a renewed sense of freedom, the kind I haven't felt since, what, when I was sixteen years old? Or maybe eight, ready for a game of kick the can.

Passing the private aircraft terminal on my left I am thrilled by the sight of an eighty-year-old Douglas DC-3 with shiny silver fuselage and wings with propellers looking more elegant than the Gulfstream jets parked nearby. Perhaps I am evoking an early childhood memory of flying in one—or maybe I saw it in a movie.

Strolling toward the main terminal, I feel the lateness

of the hour and a feather-lightness in my physical and mental being as if a wood yoke has been lifted from my shoulders and tossed onto a sacrificial bonfire. Inside, I look around for the departures monitor.

There is only one flight left to go on this day, this night, and this plane—Flight 33—is leaving... I check my watch... in forty-five minutes.

After just a moment's hesitation, I saunter up to United's check-in counter. "Any availability to San Francisco?"

She looks up at me with a puzzled expression. "You're not booked on this flight?"

"I know." I shake my head in something like abject shame. "Something came up at the last moment, no time to book a seat."

She happily clacks away at her keyboard and studies the screen. "Yes, you are. Just one way?"

I nod.

"ID and credit card?"

I oblige her.

"Any bags to check?"

"Nope."

"Would you like to book a return?"

"No."

Within seconds, a boarding card ejects from her console and with it I ascend by escalator one floor to security, nothing but my shoes to dispatch through an x-ray scan. Not three minutes later I'm sitting at the bar with a Bombay Sapphire gin and tonic in my hand and an unshakeable grin on my face.

The last flight of the evening is on time and not very full. And so, at 8:40 precisely, the small Canadian Regional Jet reverses from Gate Number 3 and taxis to the short, lit up runway.

A cute brunette with electrifying eyes, Snow White skin and sleek black hair styled into a short bob, takes the seat across the aisle from mine, throwing me a quick glance with seductive smile. And then, soon after taking off and leveling out, this gal smiles at me again. "Now that we're in the air," she says with a lyrical lilt, "where you headed, baby?"

I shrug, amused by her choice of words. "I don't know."

"You don't know?"

I shake my head, returning her mischievous smile with one of my own. "I truly don't. Until an hour ago when I wandered into the airport, I had no idea I'd be heading anywhere tonight. I caught the last flight out, on pure impulse. It didn't even matter to me where it was going."

"You're taking a powder?"

I chuckle at her lingo. "I guess you could put it that way."

She chuckles back at me. "Been thrown a curve?"

"I'll tell you this," I say. "I've wanted to run away from home way more often as an adult than I ever did as a kid."

"I know how that works," she says, nodding, her chuckle growing into a giggle. "I've done it myself more times than I can remember, starting from Kansas—twice—to unbuckle the Bible belt."

She plants her eyes directly into mine. "My name is Lulu. Pleased to meet you." Lulu thrusts her right hand at me for a shake and I marvel at the silkiness of her pale skin. "So, what happens when you arrive in Frisco?"

I shrug again. "I have no idea." By now, the gin coursing through my veins emboldens me. "Do you?"

Because, at this point, I have sort of clicked to the notion that destiny is in charge of whatever happens next in my life, not me, and here we are, hurtling together in time and space through a starry sky.

"I do," she replies with bewitching insouciance, saying nothing more.

After a few moments of silence, I follow up. "And that would be?"

"Sausalito."

"Is that where *you* are going?" I ask, more curiosity on my part rather than truly wanting to make anything more of this than two ships passing in the night.

"No. But if I was as footloose and fancy free as you

seem to be this evening, that's where I'd go to dance in my dreams."

What a way with words, I marvel. "Okay, so tell me about Sausalito."

Lulu's eyes twinkle brighter than the stars outside my porthole as she rubs her hands in glee. "It's the cat's meow."

The cat's meow! I cannot remember the last time I heard that expression, maybe watching an old movie.

She slides across the empty seat next to hers to peer out a window. "Look!" she says excitedly, pointing down. "I can see The Ranch!"

"What ranch?" I ask.

"Why, San Simeon, of course—where else? WR's stuffy old castle!"

It's hard for me to see her view from where I'm seated so I just smile and nod.

"Reminds me of a few people I once knew," Lulu explains. "But to answer your question, Sausalito is a quaint old fishing village and it's just north of the Golden Gate Bridge. It has a bees-knees view of the whole bay area and also of the San Fran skyline. Speaking of which," she adds. "I need a drink, and, specifically, I want a Bees Knees!" She glances up and down the aisle. "Where's an air hostess when you need one?" She waves the distant flight attendant down. "Ah, dearie, please mix me a gin,

honey and lemon. No? Okay, make it gin and lemonade,
I'll slum it, wouldn't be the first time." She turns back to
me. "One of my favorite states is gin-coherent."

I laugh, and order one myself. "Does Sausalito have
a hotel you'd recommend?"

"It does, and I shall," she says, delighted that I am
entertaining her suggestion. "Hotel Sausalito. Smack in
the middle of everything. Oh, and there's an ab-so-lute-ly
wonderful shop nearby you must visit."

"What kind of shop?"

"A very special shop that sells vintage photographs—
hundreds and hundreds of pictures of all kinds from the
late 1800s onward. Some of their photos are so ducky,
you just want to step inside and become part of them,
join a bygone era."

Clearly, from Lulu's retro-style clothing—a purple vel-
vet smoking jacket and a mink scarf wrapped around her
neck—she is a vintage fan.

My eyes fixate upon a silver cross that dangles just
above her cleavage. It is larger and more elaborate than
crosses I've seen. Her eyes follow mine, leading to an
embarrassing moment. "I'm looking at your *cross*," I say.

She winks. "Wouldn't matter to me wherever you're
looking, baby."

I crack a smile in appreciation of her good-naturedness.

"Where is it from?"

"It's a Coptic Cross." Lulu pats it with her fingers. "They come from Ethiopia, where they're handed down as family heirlooms and worn as a symbol of faith. Though I have my own wicked twist on that."

Somehow, I knew she would.

"Which is?"

"Ethiopia is where the first humans existed, where the human race was born." She fondles it away from her milky skin. "Do you like it?"

"I do," I say, nodding. "It looks very beautiful on you."

In one quick movement Lulu lifts the blue cord necklace over her head and slips it around mine. "Please take it," she says. "I want nothing more to do with anything that represents humanity. Better you than me."

"No, I couldn't," I say, surprised by her generosity.

"Never refuse a talisman," she winks. "And never refuse a gift from a dame."

"You're too kind," I say. "You truly are. But I could never take this from you."

"Baloney." She shakes her head. "You're not *taking* anything from me. I'm *giving* it to you."

I'm speechless, but I finally manage a *thank you* while plotting a way to slip it into her black beaded purse when she's not looking.

"It is important to me that you wear it," she says, gazing deeply into my eyes. "I just know in my bones it will help you along with your journey."

"But you don't even know where I'm going," I protest. "And for that matter, neither do I."

"And that is precisely why you need it! And maybe," she adds, "this Coptic Cross will help renew *your* faith."

"Doubt it," I say, "but thanks anyway."

Lulu reaches across the aisle and cups her warm hand over mine. "Do you know what Charlie once said?"

"Charlie?"

"Chaplin, of course."

"Of course." I chuckle, indulging her.

"Charlie said, 'Tensions are vital to life. One should never completely relax unless one wants to feel the poetry of slowly dying.'" Lulu locks her dark brown eyes into mine. "If you go to Sausalito, and happen to visit the shop I mentioned, the vintage photo gallery, be sure to get lost inside of it. And," she adds, "put your sanity aside."

By this time, because the flight is so short, and also because my sense of time seems mysteriously absent, we have already begun our descent into the Bay Area, and before I know which end is up, the plane is on the ground rolling toward a gate.

4.

Although I wanted to return Lulu's silver cross, she inexplicably disappeared before I could even say good-bye, and I soon find myself in a taxi queue, though my spacey-ness is such that I'm not even sure how I got from the plane to the taxi rank—probably due to my intake of gin from the Honor Bar, the airport, and on the airplane.

The line moves briskly and within minutes I'm ensconced in the backseat of a yellow cab.

"Where to, boss?"

"Sausalito," I say, whimsically, having nowhere else in mind.

He flips his meter and off we roll, along a highway eerily quiet this time of night, just past ten o'clock.

Interstate 101 winds into the city, becomes one with it, traffic lights and light traffic; Van Ness, Lombard—fleeting glimpses, between gaps in urban buildup, of the Golden Gate Bridge. But if I was flowing before, I'm ebbing now.

What have I done?

You might be free from life's burdens at age sixteen, but you are also not yet mature, and this is what I'm dwelling on now, the *immature* aspect of running away from home; of impulsively catching the last flight out on nothing more than a whim.

The orange vermilion arches of the magnificent suspension bridge loom ahead partly concealed by a shroud of fog rolling in from the ocean, and it somehow synapses my brain into a mad thought.

"Can you pull over?" I ask the cabbie.

"Why?" he asks suspiciously, checking me out in his rearview mirror.

What *am* I thinking? "I need to puke," I say.

"Open a window and hang out your head," he says. "Maybe the fresh air will help."

The feeling passes, though I can tell I've made the driver nervous; he eyes me in his mirror the rest of the ride to Sausalito, which isn't far, the very first exit ramp beyond the bridge, just as that quirky gal on the plane had said.

"Where in Sausalito?" he asks.

"Hotel Sausalito," I say, remembering her recommendation.

Wordlessly, he taps my destination into an iPad navigator. "El Portal," he says.

"Excuse me?"

"It's the name of the street where your hotel's at—El Portal."

A portal, I think, and I realize I never re-powered my cell phone after landing. And then I further realize I *like* it this way—*off*. And though the masochistic part of me is tempted to listen to whatever messages filled with vitriol await me on voicemail, I don't, and I determine that remaining switched off somehow empowers me, as if a transfer from techno-gizmo-interference to human brain has taken place and *I'm in charge*, despite negative energy trying to to follow me.

In other words, this is a *de*-charge, the psychological equivalent of a detox.

The cabbie cuts left just beyond a small park and pulls over. "Thirty-seven dollars," he says, half expecting me to bolt, I sense.

I hand him Ulysses S. Grant. "Keep the change."

He looks relieved. "It's a permanent solution to a temporary problem," he mumbles.

"Huh?"

"Suicide. Whatever you're feeling, dude—it'll pass."

"Excuse me?"

"Most people who jump have second thoughts right after jumping and then it's too late. That's what the survivors say, anyhow. At least think about it, dude. There's always tomorrow."

I alight without looking back into a night colored black

and pass beneath a red awning into Hotel Sausalito's lobby, small and plain, pine and faux marble, a reception counter and an elderly gent on the cusp of his third-third pulling graveyard shift. He looks up from whatever's hypnotized him on a television screen beneath his counter and startles from my unexpected presence, the lateness of the hour.

"Do you have a room available?" I ask.

He studies me. "Late check-in?" he finally says, meaning, I think, *late to check in, isn't it?*

I nod.

"Your name?" He seems poised to find me somewhere in his database.

"No, I don't have a booking," I explain. "I think I'm what you call a walk-in."

He clacks away at his keyboard while I study myself in a large, framed horizontal mirror behind him, wondering who I have become, and he snaps me back. "Got it. Two hundred, forty-five dollars plus taxes."

I trade him a credit card for a key. "Anywhere to eat around here?"

"The Barrel House." He checks his wristwatch. "But it's already closed. So is everything else around here by now."

"What time is it?" I ask.

"I just told you," he says. "Now."

5.

In my dreams, while asleep, someone is hollering at me about something, so I'm happy to wake up—daylight streaming through the curtains—even though it takes me a few long moments to figure out where I am, and when I do, I can scarcely believe what I've done, out of pocket eight hundred bucks—and climbing.

And I don't even have a toothbrush.

I turn my boxer briefs inside out and dress in yesterday's clothes and amble down the stairs.

"Is there a Starbucks around here?" I ask a lady that replaced the graveyard guy.

"Turn left on Bridgeway, first right."

Outside, I join nineteenth-century artist James Whistler's concept of a *silvery day*, stroll a pavement moist with precipitation toward the main drag and ensconce myself inside a cozy Starbucks decorated with black-and-white photographs of Sausalito in its earliest days. A latte brings me to life; back to reality, which is not such a wonderful thing this day, my phone still off and no longer feeling like an empowerment thing, more about hiding out, with nomophobia (cell phone separation) creeping in.

Caffeine cues me into working out a tentative plan: stroll around, enjoy an early lunch—I'm famished—and aim myself back to the airport for a flight home, tail between my legs.

One coffee turns into two as I watch the village come to life through a plate glass window.

Just past ten, I amble out and continue down Princess Street past a sign hanging overhead that says *Something/ Anything*, followed by another depicting the mystical winged horse, Pegasus, and then, adjacent to an alleyway, a funky house-turned-shop with a front display window featuring photographic memorabilia.

It strikes a familiar chord and takes a few seconds before… Ah, this must be the shop Lulu from the plane told me to visit.

Thinking of her, I tug on the Coptic Cross still hanging around my neck—I never took it off, slept with it—and enter The Vintage Photo Gallery. A pretty blonde female appears and I'm about to say *hello* when I realize she's not real, but just a mannequin, which provokes this fleeting thought: *Is anything really real?*

Inside, narrow aisles divide two long rows of light pinewood shelving filled with photographs categorized by subject and geographical location. I've never until this moment seen a shop like this—or so many vintage pics assembled under one roof. All of its wall space, from floor to ceiling, is covered with framed photos, an aroma of mustiness cut by incense, along with a mish-mash of lighting, retro track spots, a vintage three-way floor lamp, and Arlo Guthrie singing *Alice's Restaurant,* probably an old vinyl LP judging by the quaint crackle accompanying the lyrics from vintage stereo speakers.

Just half a mile from the railroad track, you can get anything you want from Alice's Restaurant.

And then a real human emerges from a back room. "Good morning and welcome." He is a tall, thin, elderly hippie with long gray hair tied into a pony tail, long gray beard and moustache, rose colored spectacles, and a necklace of colorful beads dangling from his neck over a tie-died tee shirt and blue jeans, God bless him for sticking with flower power and doing it true.

"Good Morning," I say.

"Looking for anything in particular?"

I shrug. "No, just browsing, thanks. Seems like a great place to look around."

He chuckles, a private joke with himself, or the world,

and I carry on, stopping occasionally to flip through rows of sepia-toned and black-and white photographs, all matted, cream-colored borders, wrapped in cellophane.

I'm probably in the shop about a half hour perusing its visual delights before I realize I've been their only potential customer, and this leaves me feeling sorry for the proprietor. Old photos are obviously his passion and, in this digital age, they most certainly enjoy less market appeal than in days gone by, which means the proprietor probably pays his rent not from sales but out of a family trust or Social Security.

Nearing the rear of the shop, I approach him where he's stooled at a high table in his small studio, happily matting photos, a whiff of marijuana in the air.

"Do you have any old photos of Mark Twain?" I ask, only half interested but curious.

"Well, they'd *have* to be old," he says with another chuckle, getting off his stool.

I follow this gangly fellow down an aisle to the *Portraits* shelf. With long skinny arms, he sifts through a stack of photos until proudly producing three images of Samuel Clemens. In one, the father of American literature is quite elderly and lying in bed reading a magazine—his deathbed from the look of it. Another image of Mark Twain is kind of blah. But the third draws me in. Clemens is standing at the far end of a pool table, pool cue in hand, with a challenging expression on his face, as if he wants to hustle the person taking his picture for a game of billiards.

"How much?" I ask.

"Seventy-five dollars each. But you can save some bread by buying all three for two hundred dollars."

The American paradox: *save money by purchasing more.* A dictum that works for some but not me this day, already in the hole for travel expenses. "I just want one."

"You'll probably be wanting more," he says, chuckling again. "Every photo in my shop is an adventure." He counts out change for a C-note and slides the photo into a large white envelope. "There's a special magic to vintage photographs, you know."

"Really? How so?"

"These photographs are not mere pictures. They are art, capable of stirring your emotions, and much more. *And...*" he adds with a big smile, "you get a Tootsie Pop with every purchase." He thrusts a mug filled with pops wrapped in different colors in front of my face.

"I haven't had one of those since I was a kid," I say. "Probably too sweet for me now."

Since I haven't made a move for one, he chooses purple and stuffs it into my shirt pocket, "Who loves you, baby?" (He must have been a *Kojak* fan.) "Enjoy being a kid again."

"Where should I have lunch?" I ask, feeling hunger pangs by now.

"My favorite is an Italian called Poggio, around the corner. Best pizza in the world."

I thank him and, with the envelope tucked under my arm (and Tootsie Pop poking from my pocket), I continue my stroll, taking in (as Lulu accurately described) a quite astonishing view of San Francisco's magnificent skyline across the bay, before backtracking to Poggio and its tantalizing aromas—garlic and basil—all the while not being able to get Arlo Guthrie out of my mind. *You can get anything you want at Alice's Restaurant.*

And it's no wonder I'm salivating since all I've eaten in the last twenty-four hours is a fruit-and-nut bar I took to the Labor Commission Hearing the morning before.

6.

order a *Funghi* pizza (with "hen of the woods mush-rooms") and a small salad and, though I rarely drink as long as the sun is out, I opt for a half-bottle of Santa Margherita pinot grigio to steady my nerves.

Awaiting my meal, to distract myself from a compulsion to power my smart phone, I pluck Mark Twain from the envelope and study his features.

Want to play?

This is a voice in my head.

I think.

And then Mark Twain's image winks at me.

I think.

Must be two sips of wine going straight to my head on a very empty stomach, I reason, returning the photo to its envelope and placing it aside as my pizza arrives, the finest pizza I've ever eaten, thin crusted and baked to perfection in a wood-burning oven.

By the time I settle my check, Poggio is bustling with patrons and, feeling good, probably an effect of the wine, I switch on my phone. About twenty missed calls—mostly from home, a few from my bar—along with a few voice-mails from both places that I decline to hear.

I saunter to the Sausalito Ferry Terminal and discover I can take a ferry to the city, and before I know it I'm aboard the M.V. Mendocino, wind whistling through my ears and seemingly saying *sanity aside*, just like the woman on the airplane. And though it is my intention to catch a cab from the Golden Gate Ferry Terminal to the airport, I enjoy the freeing experience so thoroughly that I find myself immediately re-boarding another ferry back the other way, albeit this one to Tiburon.

After alighting the ferry, strolling toward the village, I become conscious of footsteps chasing after me.

"Hey, mister!"

I turn.

"Is this yours?" He holds up the photo envelope.

"Yes, thank you."

Truth be known, I'd wanted to be freehanded—free in general—and had purposely left the photo behind for someone else to discover and enjoy. Also, truth be known, getting winked at by an image in a photograph kind of freaked me out.

But Mark Twain is apparently tough to lose, because here he is again, in my custody.

Tiburon is even cooler than Sausalito—literally, a cool breeze with a light drizzle blowing in from the bay, more sedate, less carnival-like.

So now I'm thinking—fed and refreshed—I'll stay another night, enjoy the idyllic tranquility in Tiburon, situated on the far end of a peninsula, and make the most of my bout with escapism, a runaway from reality—give everyone a chance to miss me, maybe they'll be *relieved* instead of *angry* when I eventually resurface.

An inn called Waters Edge practically sucks me into its lobby, and before I've had a chance to think it all through I'm inside a cozy room with fireplace, into which I place a self-starting log and set it alight. Then I step onto its balcony to enjoy the view of Angel Island, a nature-preserve across the water.

So now, committed to a second night away and feeling somewhat grungy, I seek a menswear store and find there isn't much to buy in this town beyond souvenir tees and sweatshirts with *Tiburon* and *Belvedere* crested upon them. Next stop: a large, well-ordered CVS pharmacy for toothpaste and a toothbrush. And then back to my room for a long, hot, sudsy bath.

Come cocktail hour I plant myself in Sam's Café next

door, a Bombay Sapphire gin martini at the bar as a prelude to moseying a few steps to Luna Blu (once in a blue moon, indeed) for a bowl of spicy cioppino (invented by the Italian piscators that fished these waters) and a glass of pinot noir.

For dessert, my Tootsie Pop. I remove its purple wrapper and indulge, having forgotten till now how good they taste, a flavor that stimulates childhood memories, such as the time I attempted, at four years old, to run away from home.

I leave the TV switched off and extinguish lights so that the only illumination is flickering cinders from remnants of the expired fireplace log and the glittery lights of San Francisco far in the distance, and a half-moon, high in the sky, beneath which I bathe upon a chair on my balcony, overtaken by a feeling that this is the center of my universe and precisely where I need to be.

Moved by so magical a setting, and by my cosmic contentment, I reenter the room to look for Mark Twain and slowly extract the photograph from its envelope, another look-see.

Want to play?

Although this seems as if it could be a voice in my mind, this time I see Mark Twain's moustache wiggle. *Sure,* I respond, feeling playful, the booze talking.

Immediately, a kind of magnetism-meets-sideways-gravity pulls at my embodiment and, feeling fearful of this extraordinary force, I resist as best I can. The pull grows stronger, way beyond what I can withstand with mere heels dug into the thin carpet, and I have no choice but surrender, eyes closed, to its superiority, spinning in some kind of vortex until—two seconds later or an hour, I'm not sure—the spinning slowly comes to a stop and I re-open my eyes... and, quite oddly, I find myself standing at the other end of a pool table across from... huh-what? Across from...

Twain is attired in a white three-piece suit, his white hair, eyebrows and moustache much wilder in person than in the photographic image I'd been holding in my hands.

"Good," he snorts, nodding. "I was thinking I'd have to lose to myself again. Go fetch yourself a pool cue."

PART TWO

7.

"Are you really…?"

"Yes, I'm really." The gravelly voice starts high-pitched and drops an octave.

"Mark Twain?"

"Call me Samuel."

"I must be out of my mind," I say, looking around the parlor in awe.

He harrumphs. "Consider that a good thing."

"Why?" I return my eyes to Mr. Clemens.

"Let's try not to overthink it, shall we? A game of pool?" Samuel pulls a Morgan silver dollar from his vest pocket. "Opening shot." He looks at me in expectance. "Call it."

Not knowing what else to say, I call it.

Samuel flips the coin onto his other hand and examines it. "Heads," he says with glee. "You lose."

I am still standing with my mouth agape, disbelieving

the scene in which I am now immersed—and in living color, not sepia-toned—while Sam steadies and shoots an opening break. Clack! His eyes zip around as he watches the balls rip in all directions and then he looks back up at me. "This is the best game on earth, and also how I get my exercise—probably ten miles a day with this cue in my hand." He lights the cigar he's been holding tight between fingers stained yellow from nicotine and impatiently puffs on it. "And it is much better than doctors for curing heartburn." He looks up. "Come to think of it, for curing *anything* known to mankind. Doctors." He shakes his hairy head with disdain. "Your shot."

"I must be dreaming," I think aloud.

Samuel nods knowingly. "In our dreams, we make the journeys we seem to make."

"Which means?"

"It means," says Samuel, "that it hardly matters whether you're dreaming, or not. All that matters this moment, in which we find ourselves together, is a game of billiards, and I strongly suggest you focus upon it rather than allow your mind to think too much." He speaks slowly, almost melodiously, as if from a musical score, and I immediately appreciate his renown as a master orator, alone on a stage for a couple of hours telling long drawn-out stories to large audiences around the world.

I choose a pool stick from a rack on the wall, chalk it up, and shoot the white ball into a small grouping of colored balls—more vividly rich in color than I've ever seen before.

"Ah, a combination shot," says Samuel. "Clearly, you believe in luck, not skill."

"Right now, I'm not sure *what* to believe."

"Next step is thinking you know, though probably you won't," he says with a snicker.

"Have I gone mad?" I ask, chalking my pool cue.

Samuel chuckles as he steps around the table to examine his next shot. "Let us consider that we are all mad. It will explain us to each other and un-riddle many riddles."

I shake my head. "I beg to differ. This isn't a riddle. It must be my imagination."

Samuel takes his shot and drops a couple balls into a pair of pockets. "Consider it a blessed thing."

"What is?"

"Why, your imagination, of course." He puffs his cigar, filling the room with an odor of cheap tobacco. "And it also means I'll win this match because you can't depend on your eyes when your imagination is out of focus. Your shot."

I aim and shoot and, feeling unfocused, I fumble. "Where are we?"

"My parlor, of course."

"I mean, where, geographically?"

"Ceaseless buzz? Hurry?" He gestures widely with both arms while new puffs of smoke rise from his cigar. "And nonstop bustle? Why, we're in New York, of course!"

I rush to a window and gaze in awe onto the street below: a trolley car and a jumble of vehicles, some horse-drawn, a scent of manure wafting up.

"When?"

"Nineteen hundred and seven." Samuel arches one of his wild brows at me. "What I'd like to know is this: from which haberdasher do you find such ridiculous garments?"

"I guess they're from the future," I say. "Before I stepped into this photograph I was in a village north of San Francisco."

"Frisco," he guffaws, blowing smoke. "A city of startling events. Do you know, the coldest winter I ever spent was a summer in San Francisco?"

"I've heard that."

Sam's facial expression turns sad. "So very tragic."

"What is?"

"Why, the earthquake, of course, last year. He shakes his head. "Almost as tragic as my losing Susy." He wipes at his eye. "Although nothing shall ever be so tragic as that."

"Susy?"

"My eldest daughter. I still grieve for her, even after ten years. I will *always* grieve for Susy—the apple of my eye." He pulls a white handkerchief from his breast pocket and loudly blows into in.

"I'm sorry."

"No, I am the sorry one," says Samuel, wiping at his nose. "Sorry for squandering the family finances on stupid inventions and bad investments. Sorry that I left my precious Susy behind when I set out on speaking engagements in faraway places to earn money for settling my debts and overcoming bankruptcy. I am so very sorry every moment of my life because Susy never would have died but for my stupidity in business."

"That's a heavy cross to bear." By reflex I reach for the Coptic Cross gifted to me; it is still around my neck.

"No one knows its burden better than I. But I did learn one thing." Samuel sucks on his cigar and blows another billow of smoke at the ceiling. "The only way I could survive was to forgive myself. And then forgive the ex-partner responsible for my bankruptcy, and anyone else I felt hard done by over the decades. Forgiveness is the fragrance that the violet sheds on the heel that has crushed it."

"Wow, what a line!"

"Of course. I'm a writer. If you're able to forgive, you remove power from the antagonist and restore it upon yourself. It is actually quite liberating." He pauses. "Susy did not join my wife and me because she was prone to seasickness. So instead she winds up with spinal meningitis. The irony." He takes a long moment to compose himself. "Doctors." He shakes his head sadly. "Children?"

I nod.

"They cause you grief sometimes?"

I nod.

"You still have them?"

I nod.

"Keep them close to you. Treasure them."

I get the message, and with it, a concern. "But, being here with you, in New York, in 1907, how can I return to my children?"

Samuel blows another gust of smoke. "I know just the solution," he says, brightening with joy.

"You do?"

He nods and winks. And when Mark Twain nods and winks, you have no doubt whatsoever about his intimate knowledge of things. "A *cock-tail.*" Samuel enunciates the word *cocktail* with great importance, as if it is something new, which perhaps for him it is.

"A little something," he winks, "I picked up not long ago in London, England. Come wander with me."

I follow Sam out of his pool parlor through a musty corridor and into a grand lounge, whose décor includes a player piano, which he switches on, and a tune begins to play.

"Is that the solution?" I ask.

"Heavens, no," Sam replies. "This is *All Aboard for Slumberville.*" He winks. "To set the right tone for a good night's sleep."

Next Samuel attacks a silver tray of ingredients and makes a major exhibition of pouring Scotch whisky, lemon juice, simple syrup and Angostura bitters into a silver shaker, adds ice, shakes it all up, and pours the mixture into a pair of crystal wine glasses, offers me one. "Drink this." He clinks his glass with mine. "As far as I can tell, and I've traveled far and wide, this concoction solves just about every malady known to mankind. Certainly, much better and less expensive than doctors and their so-called medicines." He looks both ways, as if he is expecting to be overheard, and whispers, "Those of us with any imagination either commit suicide or keep their reasoning faculties atrophied with drink."

I close my eyes, take a gulp, savor the explosion of sweet and sour swishing around my mouth, and reopen my eyelids after a few seconds.

Sam's "cocktail" does, indeed, taste very good.

But I'm *still here.* With Mark Twain. In New York City. And it's 1907.

"This continues to be very strange," I say, making my point that I have not gone anywhere at all, least of all where I belong.

"The next best thing," replies Samuel, "is steak and eggs for breakfast. But must you continue to dwell on the strangeness of your circumstance, about how or why you're in my home, or is it possible that you might simply relax and put your sanity aside?"

His question is astute, and of course it should be, because, after all, this is the great Mark Twain, and not many people get a chance to speak with him anymore. And where did I hear that phrase before, about putting my sanity aside?

"How do *you* feel about this?" I blurt.

"This?"

"My presence here."

"Stuck," he says.

"Stuck?"

"If I'm hearing you correctly," says Sam, "I am stuck inside a photograph, of all things. Which is just as ridiculous to me as it is to you."

"Why is that?"

"Because I never liked photographs, or approved of them. If a man tries to look serious when he sits for his picture, the photograph makes him look as solemn as an owl. If he smiles, the photograph smirks repulsively. If he tries to look pleasant, the photograph looks silly. If he makes the fatal mistake of attempting to seem pensive, the camera will surely write him down as an ass. One thing is for certain," he adds disdainfully, "the piece of glass it prints it on is well named a *negative*." Sam looks up to the ceiling and drains his cocktail, then returns his eyes to mine. "And here I am, like it or not, reduced to a mere image in a photograph. Maybe, for all my sins, this is my personal hell? But I'm not complaining. So long as I can drink, smoke a cigar, and play billiards, I am content."

"So why am *I* here?"

"There you go again. Stop with your poke-bogey!"

"But there must be a reason that I'm here, trapped inside a photograph with you."

"Would you prefer to be trapped inside a photograph with somebody else?"

It is a good point, and in the absence of not knowing how to respond, I remain quiet, leaving Sam to fill the silence.

"We humans don't reason, we just feel," he says. "You felt your way. So just feel your way out whenever you choose to leave."

"But how?"

"I wouldn't be in such a hurry if I were you. You may find that you'll miss me. Nothing so liberalizes and expands a man as travel, and for you to be able to journey into metaphysical realms beyond physical reality? Why, you are a very fortunate man. I could only ever achieve such a concept in my imagination, in my writing, which indeed I did, transporting a Yankee from Connecticut back to King Arthur's Court. Yet here you are, from the future, inside a photograph from the past." Sam stops to think, seeming to marvel at my predicament, as he perceives it. "Have you even considered that maybe *you* are a message to *me*? Here I am, in 1907, and a man in strange clothing visits me from the future. I could make a story of that. May I enquire as to *when* in the future you are from?"

"Over a hundred years."

Sam cocks one of his brows. "Did you hear of me before arriving here?"

"Are you kidding? *Everyone* has heard of you. You are the most famous writer in America."

"*Writer,* you say?" He eyes me with suspicion. "Not *humorist?*"

"Writer."

"Now *that's* amusing. Susy used to fret about that. All for nothing, it seems. She worried that everybody laughed at me."

"I think the last laugh is yours. I cannot even count the number of schools and parks and libraries that are named after you all around the country. Your books about Tom Sawyer and Huckleberry Finn are compulsory reading in elementary school. You are one of the most famous men in American history and *the* most famous American literary figure."

Sam looks cross, albeit with a twinkle in his eye. "Fame is a vapor, popularity an accident. The only earthly certainty is oblivion."

"Maybe," I say. "But, if so, I think you beat the system." I pause. "Hey, wait a second. Since you're dead, and I'm here with you, maybe I died." The thought anguishes me.

Sam closes one eye. "Do you fear death?" he asks sternly.

I don't answer, still trying to come to grips with the thought that I might be dead.

"Ah ha," he says. "It means you fear life. A man who lives fully is prepared to die at any time."

I start to speak but Sam harrumphs, turns his heel, and I follow him back down the woody corridor.

Upon re-entering the billiards parlor, I feel the same strange gravitational force I'd felt earlier, only this time I'm feeling it pull me the *other* direction (and just when I'd finally relaxed enough to enjoy myself), and Sam becomes more and more distant before my eyes, smaller and smaller, saying something in the way of farewell, which sounds like *for…give…ness…* And then he is just an image inside a sepia-toned photograph that I'm looking at from an upholstered armchair in my Waters Edge hotel room.

Mark Twain is standing, as before, at the far end of his pool table, motionless.

Not even a wink.

My first inclination is to believe I'd dreamt it all; that sheer exhaustion had claimed my wakefulness while I'd studied the photograph in my hands. But this was unlike any dream I had ever before experienced. More like a hallucination.

What kind of mushrooms had Poggio put on its pizza— hen of the woods?

Or maybe it was the Bombay Sapphire gin, known by some for its ability to induce phantasm, a phenomenon I discovered years ago after drinking three the same evening and dreaming wildly all night.

My next thought is the Tootsie Pop—that is, what that old hippie might have laced it with. Especially when I recall what he said when he gave it to me, something about *every photo being an adventure?*

I'm not sure whether to call him out on it or give him a hug for my mind-expanding experience.

But I do want an explanation.

8.

At 10:03 AM, precisely, I'm standing outside The Vintage Photo Gallery awaiting its hippie proprietor to open his door for business. (To return to Sausalito I had taken, not two ferries via San Francisco, but a mere fifteen-minute cab ride from Tiburon.)

An ancient Volkswagen minibus painted in psychedelic colors rounds the corner onto Princess Street and rolls to a squeaky halt in an alley space adjacent to the shop.

The owner of the gallery climbs his gangly frame out and grins widely when he sees me lurking by his entrance. "What-say?" he says. "Returning for another picture or three?"

"No," I reply solemnly. "I need to talk to you about that photograph of Mark Twain I bought from you yesterday."

"Okay, but I'm running late, so let me get the lights on and I'll be with you shortly."

As he goes through his opening rituals—switching on

lamps and such—I stroll the aisles, glancing around at various photos while taking care to restrain myself from focusing on any one picture too deeply; not taking any chances in case one pulls a Mark Twain on me.

"Okay," says the proprietor, stooped at his desk. "Lay it on me, man."

"What's your name?" I ask.

"Chem," he replies.

"Chem?"

"It's short for Alchemy."

"That's a real name?"

He shakes his head. "It's been my real name ever since I arrived at Haight-Ashbury in 1966."

"Okay, Chem," I say. "I'll get straight to the point. What was in that Tootsie Pop you gave me?"

Chem plucks one of his pops from the mug, adjusts his reading glasses, and holds it up to the light to study the wrapper: "Sugar, corn syrup, soybean oil, cocoa, whey…"

"I'm talking about your own special ingredient."

He turns from the Tootsie Pop to face me. "*My* special ingredient?"

"Exactly."

Chem shrugs, somewhat puzzled. "I don't know what you're talking about."

We lock eyes.

"I'm talking about whatever special ingredient you added to the Tootsie Pop."

He chuckles. "I didn't *add* anything, man—it's just a Tootsie Pop."

"Really, now," I say. "I'm thinking maybe you *accidentally* laced it with a hit of something from your medicine cabinet." I'm watching his eyes for a reaction, something, anything to confirm my suspicion. But he doesn't react. "What was it," I snap, trying to catch him out. "Cannabis? Mescaline? Or was it LSD?"

"Acid?" Chem shakes his head, chuckling. "Those days are long gone, man—for me, anyway, and everyone else I used to know." He throws his long arms outward, a picture of earnestness. "It was really just a Tootsie Pop."

"Then how do you explain the *trip* I took?"

"A trip? What kind of a trip?"

"The photograph I bought from you yesterday, of Mark Twain, remember that?"

"Of course, I do."

"Well, I got sucked into it."

"What do mean you got sucked into it? Sucked into *what?*"

"I think you know perfectly well."

"Know *what?*"

"Some kind of strange magnetic gravity drew me into

that photograph I bought from you. It sucked me into the image and I became part of what was going on in the picture."

Chem looks at me, a disbelieving expression, as if I'd lost my mind. "Clue me in, man. I must be missing something."

"I was *inside* the photograph," I say. "I actually *met* Samuel Clemens. And I played billiards with him."

"Far out, man!" He smiles broadly. "Reminds me of my favorite all-time band, The Doors!"

"Huh?"

"You broke on through to the other side," he sings.

"Oh, really now?"

"Of course. It originally comes from Aldous Huxley's Doors of Perception. Did you know Jim Morrison named his band after that book?" He ponders this. "I'm sure I have a photo of Jim Morrison around here somewhere." He rushes off. "Even better!" he cries from his studio.

Moments later he returns beaming and a crackling on the old stereo speakers explodes into *You know the day destroys the night, night divides the day, tried to run, tried to hide, break on through to the other side...!*

"You should-a heard them live," says Chem, slapping his thigh to the beat. "I did once. June eighteenth, 1966, at the Whiskey."

"The Whiskey?"

"Whiskey a Go Go, in LA. They—The Doors—their music, before they got famous… it was like a shamanic ritual. Experiencing them, on acid. Whoa! One of the greatest moments of my life! And then they jammed with Van Morrison!" He shakes his head. "It never got better than that. Than *The End*."

"What?

"It was always the last song they played. Never any encores. *The End*. Period." Chem is lost in his thoughts. "Wait a second!" he hollers. "I think I have a photograph of it somewhere!"

"No, no, no," I say, trying to bring him back on track. "Doors of Perception is a book about mescaline, right?"

"And peyote," Chem snaps to, nodding vigorously. "Huxley was deep into mescaline way before the sixties, one of the early pioneers of psychedelics. And Huxley borrowed his title from William Blake, who wrote, and I quote, 'If the doors of perception were cleansed everything would appear to man as if it were infinite.'" Now Chem shakes his head just as vigorously. "But you were just dreaming, man."

"It wasn't a dream," I say. "It happened *before* I went to bed. It was for real. No, *surreal*. Mark Twain even shook a cocktail for me. It tasted as real as anything."

"Groovy," says Chem. "Sounds like you bounced a reality

check, man, but I don't disbelieve you. When it comes to photos from this shop, you have to put your sanity aside."

"What did you just say?"

"I said you have to put sanity aside—why?"

"That's *exactly* what Sam Clemens told me. Wait a second, *and* the woman on the airplane."

"What woman on what airplane?"

"The woman I met who told me to come to Sausalito—and who also said I should visit your shop." I pause. "I think her name was Lulu. Do you know her?"

"Know who?"

"The woman I met. Lulu."

He shrugs. "Who the hell knows? Maybe I do, maybe I don't. I've known a lot of women. Free love. Those were the days, man—they gave it away. But offhand I can't think of anyone I know named Lulu, and I remember those days better than last week."

"It's all so weird," I say.

"I guess that's why you're supposed to put sanity aside." Chem grins. "Enjoy the experience. But then get real again. Otherwise people might start thinking you're cuckoo if you tell them you got pulled into a photograph."

"But that's exactly what happened."

"It sounds to me like you experienced something very cool, man, something truly extraordinary, so stick to your story, embrace it as part of your overall existence." He fingers his beaded necklace in thought. "Hey, maybe you should try it again?"

"Are you nuts? What are you on?"

"Just endorphins, man."

"You mean revisit Mark Twain?"

"No, no, no." Chem shakes his head vigorously. "No point. You've already done that. Try doing whatever you did, or thought you did, with a *different* photograph."

"I don't know." I consider his proposition. "It was very disconcerting. I didn't know how I was going to get back. Or *if* I was going to get back." I pause. "Have you heard of this happening to anyone else who bought photographs from your shop?"

"Not like what *you* experienced, man."

"What do you mean by that?"

"Everyone, if they're imaginative enough, finds their own level of magic in the images I sell here. In your case, you seem to have traveled in time, using one of my photographs as a portal to another dimension. Some scientists say time and space is just an illusion."

This is getting too much for me.

"It would mean," continues Chem, "you might have the ability to go back into the past. And maybe even have the opportunity to *change* things. Can you dig it, man?"

"Not so fast," I say. "If we assume what I experienced really happened, what if I go into a picture and can't get out? What if I got *stuck* there?"

He shakes his head. "Sounds like the definition of a bad trip. Which of course reminds me of the old days," he adds, smirking. "If you were really still here, physically, and your mind lived in another reality, another period in time, you'd probably end up getting committed to a madhouse." He pauses to consider his words. "Which makes me wonder if that's why some folks *are* committed to madhouses. The voices are real!" he shouts in mock horror and takes off down one of the long aisles, with me in tow, ranting, "This is cosmic, man!" I almost bump into him when he stops abruptly to pluck a picture from one of his shelves and turns around to face me. "I've got just the picture for you!"

Chem holds up a sepia-toned photograph of President John F. Kennedy and his First Lady Jacqueline. "This was taken at Dallas-Fort Worth Airport on November twenty-second, 1963, about an hour before JFK got assassinated," he explains excitedly while sucking on a chocolate brown Tootsie Pop. "If what you're saying is true, you should be able to get in there, into this picture, Dallas, November 1963, and warn Kennedy, and in so doing prevent the President of the United States from getting assassinated that day, and thereby change the course of history."

He pauses to appreciate the poignancy of his ideation. "I lost a lot of good friends, drafted into the army and shipped out to Vietnam. It was a real drag, man. Kennedy never would have allowed that stupid war to escalate like LBJ did."

"I don't know," I say, shaking my head.

"This photograph is my gift to you, to the world." He joyously thrusts it at me. "It's yours, no charge."

As if that should settle it.

"I'm not concerned about the money," I say.

"Even better." He shrugs. "Because I could really use the bread."

"You're suggesting that I just show up in Dallas out of the blue, in 1963—and warn Kennedy that he's about to be shot?"

"That's exactly what I'm suggesting, man. Listen." He points up at a corner speaker and goes quiet so we can hear Arlo Guthrie singing, *Sail with me into the unknown void.*

"And just how am I supposed to pull that off?"

"Well, first you have to get into the picture, like you did with Mark Twain, assuming that's what really happened."

I roll my eyes. "It really happened."

"Then I suggest you do exactly what you did yesterday

after leaving here, eat the same food, stay in the same room, and don't deviate from anything you did yesterday, and…"

"That's not what I meant, though point taken. What do I do when—*if*—I get there?"

"Just tell him, man."

"That he's about to be killed unless he changes his route?'

Chem nods wildly. "That's *exactly* what you need to do. Straight up. No point beating around the bush." He pauses. "Did you have anything to drink before meeting Mark Twain?"

"Bombay Sapphire."

"Botanicals." He grins. "Do the same again." He stops to think. "Oh, and you'd better have another Tootsie Pop—purple, right?"

I eye him with suspicion.

"You realize," says Chem, "if you're successful, and Kennedy doesn't get assassinated, I may not be here when you get back."

"No? Where are you going?"

"Cause and effect, man!" He throws up his hands. "Don't you know anything about time travel? So much would be different about my life, about everyone's lives, if JFK never got assassinated. I became an activist and moved to Berkeley to join the Antiwar Movement. And I was in Chicago for the Democratic convention in 1968. I even got beat-up by Mayor Daley's pigs. I should have been the Chicago *Eighth* for chrissakes! Those are life-changing experiences, man—for me, anyway. I'd probably be some-where else, doing something else."

"This is just getting more ridiculous."

"Hey, you're the one who says you traveled back in time by entering a photograph and that you shot pool with Mark Twain—and now you're calling *me* ridiculous?"

"Not you. This *situation* is ridiculous. Absurd."

"I'm actually trying to take you seriously, man, which is a hell of a lot better than what the psychiatric com-munity would do with you." Chem puts a forefinger to his head. "Zzzzzap! That's how they solve brain anomalies like yours—with meds and electrical current, maybe even a lobotomy. Here, just take this picture, keep your sev-enty-five bucks, and do whatever the hell you want with it. Happy trails, kemosabe."

9.

I do as I did the day before, stroll to Poggio for an early lunch—mushroom pizza and a salad—and return by water taxi to Tiburon, where I practically have to beg Waters Edge for the same room, 219, that I occupied the evening before.

After two nights away from home, I feel impelled to phone my family, try to explain why I must remain away for at least a third night. But I know in my heart and soul this would break the spell—or whatever's going on with me—for the important mission at hand.

Bombay Sapphire gin, dinner at the bar, a moon bathe on my balcony, and finally, at the exact same time as the evening before, I remove the photo from its envelope and gaze upon it.

Immediately, without a moment's hesitation, I am drawn into the image by a magnetic pull, my ears filling with a loud *whooshing*, and I'm abruptly traveling through some kind of portal into, I presume, another time and another place.

And all of a sudden there she is, Jacqueline Kennedy, oh so beautiful and radiant, wearing a pink suit with a pillbox hat. Jackie is standing not ten feet directly in front of me alongside her handsome husband, clothed in a dark business suit, and I am so near the president I can discern his subtly patterned striped shirt and tie, and how very youthful and vibrant they both look.

I glance around. Nearby is Air Force One, smaller than I would expect it to be, and no wonder, it is a Boeing 707, not a jumbo jet. The aroma is jet fuel. A crowd of people, many holding up banners and signs, are cheering. We are standing on the tarmac at Love Field

with an autumn breeze. JFK turns to look straight at me and startles, a bemused expression crossing his ruddy facial features.

"Mister President!" I blurt, trying my best to be heard above the commotion. "Don't...!"

But before I can utter another sound, the swarthy man in a dark suit and dark glasses that had been in the photograph standing a few feet behind the President and First Lady lunges in between them and, with a flying tackle, brings me down to hard concrete.

"Stop!" I can barely breathe and realize I have the wind socked out of me, but nonetheless struggle to continue speaking. "I have to..." I'm wheezing... "I have to... warn the President!"

By this time two goons are painfully upon me, one of them bending my arms behind my back, clasping my wrists into cold steel.

"Please listen to me!" I implore, catching my breath, finding my voice. "The President will be shot today at Dealey Plaza!"

"It's a psycho," mutters one of the U.S. Secret Servicemen to the other as I catch an upside-down glimpse of additional bodyguards bustling John F. Kennedy into a shiny black Lincoln Continental with its convertible top down, woe be he, and the country.

A moment later, I'm sitting in my hotel room chair, trembling, and staring at a glossy photograph of a smiling John and Jackie Kennedy.

This is the thought that goes through my mind:

I can do this. But I need a different image.

I excitedly phone The Vintage Photo Gallery, but of course it is closed and so it just rings and rings and rings, that old hippie doesn't even use an answering machine.

10.

After a restless night's sleep, I return by taxi to Sausalito to report my failure and upon entering the vintage photo shop its hippie proprietor trots from the back of the shop with a huge smile plastered across his face. "It's you!" he enthuses.

"I got into the picture!" I blurt. "But it didn't work." I shrug glumly. "I got pounced on by Kennedy's bodyguards before I could deliver the message to him."

Chem shakes his head, brimming with excitement. "I can't believe it's really you!"

"Huh? What do you mean by that?"

"Kennedy never got shot!"

"What?"

"The Secret Service got spooked that November day in 1963. After they got the president into the limo they put the top up and drove full speed to the Trade Mart where Kennedy gave a quick speech and flew straight back to Washington, DC! JFK was reelected in 64 and served two full terms!"

The impact of this stuns me to the core.

I changed history? Kennedy never got assassinated?

"That's amazing!" I say, incredulous. "How has the world changed?"

"Beats me." He shrugs. "All I know is, it probably didn't change mine, but there's no way of me knowing for sure, except I'm here right now."

"What do you mean? How can that be?"

"I followed my heart. We activists protested JFK in Chicago over Vietnam...."

"You mean the Vietnam War escalated?"

"Way out of control, man. And then Gene McCarthy ran against Nixon and lost, and it got worse. But *you* tell *me*—is that different from what you were talking about yesterday?"

"Wait a second. Did Nixon Watergate himself?"

"Huh?"

"Watergate."

"What's that?"

"Wait a second, did Nixon have to resign?"

"What are you talking about?" Chem expresses puzzlement. "Nixon never resigned. He served two terms and was succeeded by his Vice President, Ronald Reagan."

"What about Jimmy Carter?"

"Jimmy who?"

"Wait a second," I say. "So, things really *did* change!"

"If you say so, man."

"Did the Soviet Union fall?"

He nods. "And then Russia got strong again."

"Nine-eleven?

"Yes, and U.S. military involvement in Afghanistan and Iraq." He shakes his head in awe. "I didn't even realize there was a parallel dimension based on your time traveling into photos until you returned to my shop yesterday after buying a photo of Mark Twain the day before. Then it clicked. And here you are again!"

My mind is now completely boggled—and then alarmed. "What effect might this have on *my own* existence," I say. "On my own family?"

"Who knows, man?" Clem shrugs. "Oh, and there's something else."

"What else?"

"You were in the news."

"Me? Why?"

"They thought *you* were the intended assassin that day. You got away, just disappeared. And I didn't even realize till yesterday," he marvels, "that it was *you* they were looking for!"

"*Who* thought I wanted to kill Kennedy?"

"Everyone!" Chem swings around, eyes wild with excitement. "The story goes like this: Someone—*you*—suddenly appeared out of nowhere in front of the President and the First Lady and started shouting like you were about to attack JFK, and the Secret Service jumped into action to subdue you. You hollered something about shooting the President. Your description—just the way you look right now—even appeared in the newspapers!"

"Holy crap!"

"It's cool, man—I don't think they're looking for you anymore." He shakes his head. "That was a long time ago, and anyway, they'd expect you to be a lot older, so everything's copasetic."

"I need to make a call." I power my phone and connect to my home number.

And it rings!

I hold my breath, my heart thumping hard.

"Where the hell are you!" It is *my wife's voice*.

I disconnect. "Some things never change," I say just above a whisper, thinking aloud. "You said you don't *think* they're looking for me anymore?"

"They never had a name, just a description," says Chem, watching me closely. "Some Internet web sites even say you were a time traveler because of your clothes."

"My Tiburon sweatshirt?"

He studies it, unsure. "That is way ahead of its time in 1963."

"You mean to tell me JFK served two full terms and everything's the same as if he'd been assassinated?"

"The first time I heard he was supposed to have been assassinated was yesterday, man, from *you*. Kennedy died a long time ago, by the way, pretty soon after he was out of office. Turned out, he wasn't a well man."

"What about his brother, Robert?"

"What about him?"

"Did he get shot, too?"

"Not that I'm aware of."

"Did he run for president?"

The old hippie scratches his head. "Why would he have done that? In any case, nobody would have voted for another Kennedy."

"What about Teddy? Chappaquiddick?"

"Huh? What's that?"

"A small island near Martha's Vineyard."

His expression remains blank.

"I need to sit down and take this all in." I look around, find a plain wooden chair, seat myself the wrong way around, resting my arms on the back of it.

"I got really spooked by you yesterday," Chem whispers.

"I don't think we should be messing with history, *if* that's what's really going on here."

"You don't believe that JFK was assassinated?"

"He *wasn't* assassinated. But I believe you *think* he was."

I look him hard in the eye. "I got news for you, buster. You and I *already* messed with history. And it was *your* idea."

"In your dreams," says Chem. "You came in here, said you got pulled into a picture of Mark Twain I'd sold you the day before. Then you said JFK had been assassinated. I thought you were screwy, man, and I found a photo to show you he had been perfectly safe in Dallas. You left my shop with it without even paying. I almost called the pigs."

"No, no, no, no, no. You *gave* me that photo. Your *gift to the world*, you said."

Chem shakes his head. "And then after that I Googled *JFK* and *Dallas* and *November 1963* and came up with a picture of *you*, laying flat-out on the tarmac!"

Now I'm suspicious. Surely, Chem is playing some kind of sick practical joke on me—and I bought it, hook, line and sinker!

"Mind if I look around a little bit?" I ask, smirking.

He hesitates a moment. "I suppose it's okay. But be careful, man." He closes an imaginary lid with his hands, arms outstretched. "I don't want any more trouble."

I move from aisle to aisle, examining various stacks of photographs. At the *Military* section, marked *World War II*, my eyes inadvertently fixate on a black-and-white image of smiley men and women in military garb looking straight at me or whomever took their picure. And then, before I know what's happening, it *is* me they're looking at, because I'm *there*, with them, pulled right out of the shop and into the photograph, nothing to do with mushroom pizza or Bombay Sapphire gin or purple Tootsie Pops or anything else.

11.

'm standing on some kind of wooden bridge in the wilderness facing a dozen uniformed men and women all gawking at me gaily, as if I am expected, or maybe I'm the entertainment; a guy on the far right wearing a military crush cap is poised to play the accordion, so happy they all seem—am I supposed to sing?

I expect him to play *You can get anything you want at Alice's restaurant,* because that's what I hear in my mind, even if the aroma is onion fields.

But he doesn't. Instead, he freezes in disbelief—and the expressions of the others transform into grimaces and scowls, the women gasping, and the men shouting.

I turn and run but they chase me down and I wind up spread-eagled onto muddy grass. Makes me think of Dallas 1963. "Dammit—not again!"

"Don't you know," the tallest man hollers, a heavy German accent, "trying to escape is punishable by death!"

I zero in on the Nazi insignia decorating his collar. "Oh, shit," I say. "Where the hell am I now?"

A couple gals chuckle, as if I truly *am* the entertainment, not a singer but a stand-up—in this case *lie-down*—comic.

"You are home," says one of the amused women.

"No, I'm not," I say, looking up at their apple-cheeked faces.

"Your *new* home," adds another, giggling.

And now the tall male German is pointing a cocked Luger at my head.

"No, no, Horst!" One of the women protests. "Not here, this beautiful place!"

Horst shoots her a lusty leer as if to say *what's in it for me?* And, satisfied by her return grin, re-holsters his weapon.

"We take him back."

"Back where?" I ask.

"The work camp."

"No friggin way!" I yell. "This is all a huge mistake!"

"Yes," replies Horst. "*You* are part of the mistake that *we correct*. Have you not tried to escape?" he adds.

The irony. Because that is precisely what I had done by taking the last flight out.

"But I don't belong here," I say. "I don't belong in a work camp!"

They all laugh.

But their good humor ends right there and the men bundle me across a field to a grey-blue bus, push me to its rear and corner me into the backseat. The engine turns—I smell diesel—and we rumble along silently. It appears I have disturbed their afternoon of relaxation in the countryside.

About twenty minutes later an austere rectangular building comes into view. It has a tower at its center over a tunnel-like entrance, wide enough for a train, and indeed, as we roll nearer, I see railway tracks running straight through it.

The bus swings into the building's forecourt and brakes to a halt in front of a gaggle of uniformed guards.

"You are lucky this time," whispers Horst, fingering

his holster. "You try to escape again, I kill you myself for sure."

They push me toward the door and I lose my footing and tumble out onto the cold ground, whereupon one of the assembled guardsmen stomps over to my sprawled self and kicks me in the stomach, leaving me to retch uncontrollably while they laugh. A whistle is blown, signaling an end to such mirth, and I am scooped up and marched through a gate of wrought iron ornately stenciled ARBEIT MACHT FREI.

Work sets you free.

Where have I heard that before?

Further on, past several murky brick buildings, they stop and fling me inside.

Inside, skinny men are squashed together like sardines in bunkbeds more like shelves, stacked four-high to the ceiling.

"Where. Am. I?" I ask, nearly frozen with fear, immediately nauseous from a horrible stench.

Says a shirtless man with an unwelcome six-pack (and I'm not talking beer): "Oy vey. Welcome to Auschwitz."

I look around, disbelieving, feeling a cold clamminess. Someone squashed onto a shelf of a bed is groaning, another praying softly, and I refocus my eyes on the frail being in front of me. "Who are you?"

"We are the *untermenschen*." As he speaks I note that his teeth are various shades of brown to black, some missing, some loose.

"Who?"

"It is what the Nazis call us, meaning 'undesirable sub-humans.'"

"You look like you haven't eaten in a month."

He nods. "Yes, it is true we undesirables eat very little. This is mostly because they don't give us much—some watery soup for lunch, a piece of black bread with a little marmalade for dinner. And partly because nothing here is very appetizing. But at least," he adds, with a wry smile, "we don't have to worry about obesity."

"That's looking on the bright side."

"Here's the bright side: if we catch a rat, we build a small fire, roast it and celebrate a decent meal. In this place, if you don't look on the bright side, you might as well be dead. The Nazis help with that, too. Follow." Unsteadily, he leads me to the doorway, grabbing my elbow for support, and points across the camp. "Way out there."

"What where?"

"You cannot see. But it's there, we know. Our people are taken there. For showering, they say. Hundreds of them at a time. Men, women, children. But no people ever come back. Do you know why?"

I have an idea about this, but I don't wish to venture it.

"They don't come out," he answers his own question, "because they are turned to gas."

"Gas?"

"Smoke is gas, no? Whenever people go in, a short while later smoke comes out. It rises from the distance. A *lot* of smoke. The people, they never come out. Except as gas. See that other building way down there?" He points to a structure about a quarter mile away. "That's a laboratory. If given a choice, always choose the smoke building."

"Because?"

"Because the monster who runs it, Doctor Mengele, conducts terrible, terrible experiments, often on children. He especially likes twins. Twin children. And he especially likes *conjoined twins*. And sometimes he conjoins them himself. Without anesthetic."

I recoil in revulsion.

"That's why we don't complain about food," he says with a hint of irony in his smile. "At least we're not conjoined with one another." He gestures at the others around him. "And we haven't been turned to smoke. And I stand up to them because I don't fear death. That, they cannot handle."

He steps back to eye me up and down. "Do you need a bunk?"

Do I need a bunk? "No, I need to get the hell out of here! I think I need to return to where I came from."

"Where might that be?" His smirk suggests everyone in this barracks would like to return to where they came from.

"If I told you," I say, "you'd think I was nuts."

"If I told you what *my own eyes* have seen, right here in this camp of death, you'd think *I* was nuts. By now there's *nothing* I won't believe. And no way I'll never not see what has happened here in nightmares the rest of my life."

I study his vacant, sad eyes, and in them I see it is true.

"I'm from the future," I say.

He nods, seeming to somehow understand. "How far in the future?"

"About seventy years."

"That does sound crazy." He studies me, unsure. "The Nazis rule the world?"

I shake my head. "They lost the war. Hitler killed himself before it ended. Everyone found out what they did—in here and in other death camps like this one. Most of the people who run this place end up getting hanged for war crimes."

"Excuse me?" He cocks his ear guided by bony fingers closer to my mouth.

I repeat what I said.

He is shaking now, riveted to every word, his eyes

filling with tears. He reaches out, weakly, with two skinny arms to shake me. "Are you certain?"

"Absolutely certain."

His weeping intensifies. "Until this moment," he says, sobbing, tears gliding freely down both cheeks, "I thought I was all cried out. But these…" he wipes at his tears and holds them above his head, studying them. "These are tears of *happiness*."

He rubs his eyes dry, poises himself and asks, "Seventy years from now humans can travel in time?"

I shake my head. "No. Well, maybe, considering I'm here talking to you right now. But my experience is just a fluke. It seems that I somehow get pulled into old photographs."

"Photographs you say?" He scratches his head. "That does sound nuts." He considers this, looking me square in the eye. "Say, if you can travel in time, through a photograph, why don't you find an old picture of Adolph Hitler before he becomes Der Fuhrer—and *kill* him?"

I return his eye gaze, not knowing what to say, but recalling to myself my encounter with JFK in Dallas.

He shakes his head, launching new tears this way and that. "You have no idea the suffering I've seen. Maybe you've read about it, maybe you've heard about it. But you have no idea what suffering *is* until you actually *ex-*

perience it with all of your senses in a place like this for days, weeks and months, even years on end. It starts off in slow motion, like you can't believe it's really happening. But over time you get more and more numb until you have almost no feeling at all, about anything."

I had stopped a man—JFK—from getting killed. And now I could potentially stop a man—one of the most evil of men in recent history—from remaining alive long enough to cause widespread suffering; from causing a world war that would lead to the deaths of sixty million people.

"Feh!" says the prisoner, looking over my shoulder. "Too late."

"Huh?" I turn to see a most ominous sight: two stern-faced soldiers wearing stiff woolen uniforms embroidered with swastikas marching straight at me.

This is where that magnetic pull is supposed to pull me the hell out of the picture, right?

Wrong.

It doesn't.

I turn and run, hopefully to give that magnetic pull I'd been feeling in situations like this a head start, or maybe just to buy some extra time to get it going. Or maybe just to get away. But there is nowhere to go or to hide in this horrible place. The uniformed goons chase me down and the only pull I feel is two burly soldiers dragging me out of the crowded barracks onto a hard dirt ground covered in ash, which not only soils my clothes but also gets up my nose, which gives me a feeling of revulsion when I realize I am breathing *human* ash.

And I'm thinking, holy crap, if these ugly goons remove me from the *scene* of the photograph I'll *never* get back to where I belong.

They drag me through a large puddle, the bastards, so now I'm soaking wet and muddy as they continue to pull me into to a building sign-posted thus: *Blok 11.*

Once inside the front door, the dragging continues down a dark moldy corridor, until they stop and scoop me up and push me hard into a dank windowless cell. One pulls out a large metal key and locks the barred gate, and they both depart.

There is nowhere for me to sit inside this tiny closet of a room, let alone lay down, just a cold cement floor, not even a toilet, which explains a pile of human excrement in a far corner coupled with puddles of urine, and blood, and a stench like I've never smelled before. All I have for company are wails and groans from other such cells.

And here I wait.

And wait.

And wait.

12.

I am hungry. But mostly I am thirsty. After what seems an eternity, a new pair of soldiers clad in grey-green tunics appear and wordlessly bundle me further along the low-lit corridor, down a flight of stairs to basement level, damper dankness, and into a room illuminated with a single naked light bulb and furnished with nothing more than two plain wooden chairs and, nearby, a long steel bar hanging by chains from the ceiling.

I have no idea what this is, nor do I wish to know.

The guards roughly sit me in one of the chairs and, moments later, in unison, snap to attention with dual salutes when another uniformed man with ape-like facial features struts in and regards me with a smile that displays big teeth from receded gums, which accentuate his simian countenance.

"I am Herr Boger," he announces in a tone that implies I am supposed to know who he is, and maybe even I'm supposed to revere his presence because my bewildered expression seems to irritate him.

"From Schutzstaffel," he adds, as if that should settle the matter.

His appearance is so preposterous that it brings to mind the old television series *Hogan's Heroes*, kudos to central casting, though I never could understand, like Rod Serling, how Nazis could be the basis for a situation comedy.

"Where's Schutzs-whats-it?" I say, thinking it is a place, though it makes me think of Sergeant Schultz, that TV show's corpulent and comical chief guard, known for this recurring line: "I know nothing."

Herr Boger's smile disappears into a grimace of tight thin lips until he parts them to utter, in a staccato voice, "Schitzstaffel is not a town, you *schwinehund*. It is an *honor* to serve in the SS. And *I* will ask the questions, not you."

It takes all my fortitude to stifle a laugh, such a character this dark ape-like man is, no blond Aryan, he—how'd *he* manage to slip into the Reich? And I think he senses my amusement.

"Do you know why they call me *The Tiger of Auschwitz*?" he asks.

I can no longer help myself and, since he seems more like a monkey than a tiger, I burst out laughing in response to his insecure bluster.

Herr Boger looks up at the guard to my left and nods whereupon the goon socks me hard on the side of the head with his ham-hock of a fist, and I fall off the chair, hitting the ground with a thud.

"Owwww! That hurt!"

Now it is Herr Boger who expresses mirth, a whistle of a laugh that sounds more like a hissing chimpanzee than a human being. "You think *that* hurt?" he mocks. "It is nothing compared to the Boger Swing." Herr Boger gestures with a limp wrist at the steel bar hanging from chains. "My own invention," he adds with a twinkle in his eye, in case I didn't immediately associate his name with a swing; *this* swing, *his* swing.

I say nothing, not wishing to provoke further physical violence upon myself.

Herr Boger nods with pride at the contraption to which he claims fame. "We strip you of all your clothes and hang you with your head down, your buttocks up, and your hands manacled beneath your knees. Next, we swing you around the pole. Every time you make a full circle we whack your buttocks with a crowbar. At the end, you are a bloody pulp and nothing more than a sack of disjointed bones. Maybe you would like to feel for yourself?"

"I'd rather not."

"Excellent. So, you will answer my questions."

"I would be delighted to do so," I say. "I have nothing to hide. What exactly would you like to know?"

"How did you get into our work camp?"

"Now that's a cruel lie," I say.

"What cruel lie?"

"Calling this a work camp."

He nods at the goon to thump me again.

"Okay, okay," I say shielding my head. "I arrived by photograph."

"Excuse me?"

"You won't be excused," I say. "But to answer your question, I inadvertently happened upon a photograph of a group of people having a day out in the woods, and as I was looking at the image it pulled me in and I became a part of it. The group of people pounced on me, pushed me into a stinky old bus, and plopped me in a barracks where I started chatting with one of your prisoners in the photo—he told me I'm in Auschwitz—and then your guards arrived on the scene and now here I am, with you." I'm still rubbing my sore jaw.

Herr Boger studies me with skepticism, glancing at the guard and, it seems to me, about to ask him to thump me again for telling, to his narrow mind, so audacious a tale.

"I know that what I'm saying is hard to believe," I

say. "But I'm telling you the truth."

The SS officer arches an eyebrow, a thin smile, perhaps intending to indulge me, for a few moments anyway. "How does that work, this *pulling*?"

"That's what *I'd* like to know," I say. "It just happens." I throw my arms up in frustration. "I have no control over it. It is not my choice to be here. It was the photo that seems to have *chosen me*. I don't want to be here. In Auschwitz. I shouldn't be here. It was only an accident."

"Only an accident," he echoes, glancing at the ham-fisted guard again.

"Yes, and I'd like to leave."

"Ha! I bet you do." Boger snorts. "Why should I believe you?"

I shrug. "All I can say is, it happened twice before this, with other photographs."

He thrusts his eyes into mine, as if thinking, *Aha, got you.* "Explain."

"The first time it happened I got sucked into an old photograph with Mark Twain."

Herr Boger sits poker-faced.

"I thought so," I say. "You don't strike me as being particularly well-read."

Fortunately, he is either deep in thought (assuming deep

thought is possible for him) or my irresistible irreverence has gone over his ape-like head.

"And the other time?"

"I went back to 1963 to…"

"Halt!"

I stop mid-sentence.

"*Back* to 1963?" he says, eyes popping.

"Yes, I wanted to…"

"It is not 1963 yet. Nineteen sixty-three is…" he counts with his fingers, left hand, right hand, left hand, right… "Twenty-years later than *now*." He has a new thought after digesting this. "So, you say you are from the *future*?"

I nod vigorously. "That is exactly right. I'm not just entering photographs but also, by extension, traveling in time and space."

Now Herr Boger is perplexed. "Have you put all sanity aside?"

"Funny you should say that," I say. "*Sanity aside*, I mean. I've been hearing that phrase a lot lately."

"Take off your shirt!" Herr Boger commands.

I shudder, fearing I've been too flippant once again. *The Boger Swing?*

With some trepidation, I pull the Tiburon sweatshirt over my head.

"Give to me," Herr Boger demands.

I hand it to him.

Herr Boger twists the garment around to feel its microfiber texture and inspect the label, its fabric—rayon and polyester—and origin, China. He looks up at me, straight into my eyes, back down at the garment, up at me again, spins around, clicks his heels, and wordlessly leaves the room. And I realize he may be smarter than he looks.

The pair of goon-guards trade puzzled glances, seemingly unsure about what they should do next. So, we all wait in silence.

Soon we hear a clop clopping down the corridor and Herr Boger reappears, this time accompanied by another officer, uniformed but hatless, mostly bald on top with a goofy fringe of hair from ear to ear backside of his head.

The guards stiffen to even greater attention than before, suggesting the presence of a chieftain.

This new addition to the Boger Swing Room regards me with a smirk. "*Zukunft Mann?*" he says.

"Huh?"

"You say you are from the future?" He regards me skeptically from head to toe and up again, planting his eyes into mine. "Who wins?"

"Wins what?"

"The war, of course."

"Don't ask," I say.

"I demand to know!" He glances at Herr Boger, obviously his stooge.

"Yes, we demand to know!" Herr Boger echoes.

"You won't like the answer."

"My name is Maximilian Grabner," the new guy says, eyeballs popping. "Do you know who I am?"

I shake my head. I really don't. Nor do I wish to know. "Sorry, no."

"I am Gestapo and chief of the political section in this camp. I have power to execute you this moment!" As if to prove his point, Grabner struggles to remove a Luger pistol from his hip, and after he finally manages to free the weapon from its buttoned holster, he aims it at my head from several inches away.

"Please don't shoot," I say. "It won't change anything. The Germans will still lose and you'll have one more murder to answer for."

Herrs Grabner and Boger swap worried looks.

"What will happen to… to *me*?" Herr Grabner asks, re-holstering his weapon with a sweaty palm.

"I don't know about you, specifically," I say. "I've never actually heard your name till now, sorry. But I can tell you—and I hope you don't take offense to this—most of the officers in this camp will be hanged for their execution of prisoners and other crimes against humanity."

Herr Boger begins to tremble. He even appears to have peed himself, judging by a widening stain on the crotch of his thick woolen trousers.

"Can this be... *changed?*" asks Herr Grabner, returning my shirt to me.

"It's probably too late," I say, shaking my head while putting my shirt back over my head. "All I can advise, from this point on, is that you should treat your prisoners well, feed them properly, and..." I point at the Boger Swing... "I'd get rid of *that* if I were you. Oh, and stop the gassing."

"You know about the gassing?"

"Zyklon B?" I say. "Everyone will know about the gassing after the war ends. It will disgrace Nazism, the Reich, even in Germany. And it's the main reason most of you get hanged."

Herr Grabner turns to Herr Boger and clucks, "I must tell Der Fuhrer!"

The two uniformed comics salute one another and Grabner clicks his heels one last time before departing, while this thought crosses my mind: *these* are the bozos in charge of running Auschwitz, running The Third Reich? Little wonder the Germans lose, their so-called "superior race" comprised of retards and lunk-heads.

Remaining behind, Herr Boger sits down in a chair wringing his hands.

"If you show me some photographs," I say to him gently, "I may be able to give you advice on how to stay alive after the war ends."

"Yaa?" Herr Boger asks anxiously. "What photographs?"

"Any photos you might possibly have," I say. "Maybe on your desk?"

Herr Boger considers my request for a long moment. Then he pulls out his wallet and plucks from it a photograph, which he unfolds and studies, bringing a smile to his face as he turns the image to face me. "This photo will do?"

It is a black-and-white photo of boys, about the age of twelve or thirteen, all in uniform, all sporting swastikas.

"The Hitler Youth, nineteen-twenty-six," Herr Boger explains, primping himself with pride. "I'm an old-timer in the Nazi movement."

"May I hold it?" I say.

Herr Boger hands the photograph to me, falling for my ruse through sheer vanity. "It is one of my dearest memories," he adds, wiping a tear from his eye.

Holding the old frayed snapshot with both hands, I relax my whole being and focus on the image, closing my eyes, silently praying to be pulled into it.

13.

I now find myself in the midst of children. Uniformed boys. They are all quiet and listening to an orator, so very hypnotized they are that they don't even notice my unexpected presence among them. And then they are chanting in German with great enthusiasm, arms out-stretched, saluting. And I realize I have gone into Herr Boger's photograph, as I had hoped, outfoxing the dim-witted SS officer.

But the issue still remains: *How do I get back to Sausalito?*

And then, just like that, I am standing inside The Vintage Photo Gallery and its elderly hippie proprietor is staring at me, eyes wide with awe.

"You disappeared into one photo and came out of another!" Chem blurts, stooping down to pick up a photo on the floor of a Hitler Youth gathering in nineteen-twenty-six—the same image Herr Boger had shown me.

"You saw it happen?" I say.

"With my own eyes." He is clearly stupefied by the experience. "First you were here. Then you weren't. And now you're here again. And this photograph literally *flew* off the shelf. I didn't even know I *had* this photo. What a gas!"

I shake my head. "Don't say that word."

"What word?"

"Gas. You have no idea what I saw, what I felt." I shudder at the thought. "I was in Auschwitz. I got apprehended by Nazi goons and dragged through the ash of cremated victims. And then I was about to be tortured on some sort of barbaric swing!"

"Bummer," he says.

"*Bummer? Bummer?* What I just experienced is *way* beyond *bummer.* I've never been so scared, and disgusted, but mostly scared, my whole life." I glance around. "Do you happen to have any photographs of Hitler before he was famous?"

"That was the most amazing thing I've ever... *what's that?*" Chem squints his eyes at me. "*Why?*" he asks suspiciously.

"Hitler. When he was young." I twirl around, glancing down aisles, eyeing category signs.

"You're not thinking...?"

I swing back to face Chem and snap, "That's *exactly* what I'm thinking. If I could save Kennedy, I can save *the world*. From Hitler."

"So, you're thinking you want to... to...?"

"Yes. I want to kill him. I need to stop Hitler before he comes to power and instigates the Holocaust."

The hippie shakes his head vigorously. "I don't know if I can be a part of that, man. *Make love not war.* That has always been my mantra."

"Hitler made war! What I'm talking about doing will *stop* a major war from ever happening and save sixty million lives!"

"Yeah, man. But the idea of killing a living human being..." Chem turns around and walks away.

"You are opposed to killing Hitler?" I call after him. "Are you friggin' kidding me? Have you no idea of the murder, mayhem and misery he wrought on mankind? Hitler wasn't a human being—he was a tyrant, a mass murderer! Trust me, there's *nothing* like *being there* to understand that if I can kill Hitler, it is my utmost responsibility to do so—and because you started all this, you must help me."

The old hippie spins on his heel to face me. "I've never subscribed to musterbation, man." He pauses and then yowls, "Heinrich Hoffman!"

"Who-what?"

"Heinrich Hoffman was a famous German photographer. On August 2nd, 1914 Hoffman took a photo in the Odeonsplatz, a large square in Munich. He later discovered that Adolph Hitler was in the crowd and his camera caught Hitler's image in the photograph. At that time Hitler was only twenty-five years old."

"Do you have it?"

"Of course. It's a classic. Hoffman went on to become Hitler's personal photographer. Did you know it was Hoffman's photographic studio in Munich that Hitler first met Eva Braun?"

I didn't.

"She was Hoffman's personal assistant," Chem continues, "and…"

"I don't give a crap about Eva Braun! Let's get on with it. Also, I'll need a weapon. Preferably a gun. Do you have one?"

"Me?" He thumbs himself, aghast. "You must be joking, man. I've been for gun control my whole life."

"What about a knife?"

"I have a Stanley knife for matting photos. I call it Stan. But as a matter of principle I cannot allow Stan be used for the purpose of harming anyone."

"Even Hitler?"

Chem nods his head resolutely. "I would never do that to Stan."

"It's an inanimate object," I say.

"Even inanimate objects are made of living molecules."

"Oh, you're a big help," I say with sarcasm. "You're the one who got me into this."

Chem shakes his head. "I sell photographs, man, and that's it. The rest is all *you*."

"That's just great," I say. "You tell me every photo of yours is an adventure, and when I get pulled into the biggest adventure of my life—against my will, I might add—there's suddenly this big friggin' disclaimer. 'I sell photographs and that's it,'" I mimic. "Well, as of right now, JFK never got assassinated—and you're as much responsible for that, this wrinkle in history, as I am."

"That's what *you* say," he says. "As far as I know, JFK *never was supposed to get* assassinated and never did. It's in *your* mind, and I only know that you changed history because *you* say so." He pauses. "And maybe because I saw you disappear and reappear."

I roll my eyes. "Whatever you say. But just tell me this: Where can I buy a knife around here?"

"Why do you need to do this?"

"Because I *can*. Whatever you might know about Auschwitz is from history books and photos and movies.

But you haven't *been there*, felt it, smelt it—*suffered* from it. I got hit!"

"Hit?"

"Slugged in the head."

"Oh, so this is personal now—you want revenge?"

"No." I consider this, reflecting what I saw with my own eyes. "I need to make sure Auschwitz never happens. Period."

"Good luck with that."

"What are you talking about? It was *your* idea that I go back in time and stop Kennedy from getting assassinated."

"I don't remember that!"

"Because I stopped it from happening!"

"So you say."

"We're going in circles. Just find me that photo of Hitler in 1914 and I'll go find my own weapon."

14.

Across the street from The Vintage Photo Gallery is Scrimshaw Gallery whose mustachioed proprietor tells me he stocks the largest collection of William Henry knives in the country. I don't need anything so fancy as a knife made with mammoth tusk or turquoise, but it looks like I have no choice—until I notice a six-inch dagger. Even better, this particular *folding* dagger *snaps open* sideways at the touch of a button.

"Tell me about this one," I ask the proprietor.

"It's called The Godfather," he replies. "Made a hundred percent from aircraft aluminum by a company called Pro-Tech.

"Lethal," he adds, as if reading my mind.

I snap it open and fold it closed, open, closed.

"I'll take it," I say, handing him plastic.

"It comes with a handsome box," he says.

"Never mind the box." I slip the dagger into my pocket. "I'm taking it to go."

Moments later, I re-cross the street and reach for the handle on the shop door. It won't turn. I try the handle again. And then I realize that dang old hippie locked it!

I bang on the door.

He doesn't answer.

I bang on it again, harder. "Open up, Chem!" I holler. "I know you're in there!"

Still nothing, though I can see he hasn't left the premises because his colorful VW minibus is still parked outside.

"I'm not leaving!" I holler, louder than before. "Unlock the door, Chem, or I'll break it down!"

Finally, he reappears, looking somewhat embarrassed as he sheepishly tries to quiet me with his hands, arms outstretched. "All right, all right, man. Cool it. I've got neighbors. Do I need to call the fuzz?"

"Screw your neighbors. And the fuzz. I'm serious. Did you find the picture?"

He nods. "Uh-huh."

"Okay, let's do this."

"You know, this whole thing is turning into a drag," says Chem. "I thought maybe you'd just leave so I can get back to my life, and my pictures."

"You kidding me? Whether you want to believe it or not, it is *your* pictures that are responsible for this. It has become your duty to assist me. This is something that must be done."

Chem spins around and I follow him to his studio where he whips around to face me with an image in hand. "See here." He points to a young man sporting a Beatle haircut and a Charlie Chaplin moustache smack in the middle of a huge crowd. "Take note that there are thousands of people around him doing their mob mentality thing," he says. "They are capable of tearing you to shreds, like a school of piranhas. You may never get out of there alive."

"I got out of Auschwitz alive," I say. "And along the way I figured out how to get out of sticky situations like that. I just need another picture of yours to take with me."

He looks at me with suspicion, as if I'm trying to steal one of his precious photographs. "Why?"

"Once I leave the scene of the photo I entered, I need another photograph as a portal to get back here. And please give me something that will provide pleasant relief. After killing Hitler, I think I'll deserve it."

He winks. "I know just what you need to bug out of there and have a good time." He strides down one of his long aisles and selects an additional photograph, which he slips into one of his white envelopes and hands to me.

"I'll like it?" I say.

"Trust me," he snickers.

"Okay, let's do this right now, before I come to my senses." I pat The Godfather dagger in my pocket and I belt my escape-clause-of-a-photograph into the small of my back.

"Hold on, bro," says Chem. "You can't go there looking like that."

"What do you mean?"

"You'll look way out of place. Here, take this." He hands me a wool overcoat and a fedora hanging on an old wooden hat-and-coat stand.

Now I'm ready.

Time to stop Hitler.

Holding the famed Odeonsplatz photo with both hands, I focus my eyes upon Hitler, around whom Chem has drawn a circle.

Nothing whooshes.

I relax and close my eyes.

Still nothing.

I reopen my eyes to see the old hippie standing in front of me.

"Maybe you need a Tootsie Pop?" he says helpfully.

"Won't hurt," I reply. "Purple."

I unwrap the pop and suck on it impatiently.

The sucking sensation in my mouth somehow extends

to a sucking sensation all around me... stronger, stronger, STRONGER—and all of a sudden, after a *whoosh*, I am standing in Odeonsplatz, Munich, a *platz* crammed with buoyant Bavarians dressed in suits and hats, all celebrating the beginning of World War I.

It is an electrifying event, full of energy—negative masquerading as positive—and much body odor.

15.

Swimming my way through a sea of people, I make my way to where a young Hitler is supposed to be, not far from a large cement monument of a lion. I get to where I think he is but I don't see him, so I continue to push through the throng, stepping on toes and bouncing off people as if I'm a steel ball inside a pinball machine, sound effects courtesy of guttural curses in German showered upon my motioning self.

Hitler should be distinctive, the only man sporting a toothbrush moustache and a Beatles-style haircut. But I still don't see him anywhere. I resist a temptation to call out *Hey Adolph!* Because, armed with only a knife, I definitely need an element of surprise to accomplish my mission.

So, I spin around and crush through more political revelers—a stench of body odor—in search of my target.

And then I see him.

Adolph Hitler.

His mouth is smiling, his eyes are a-twinkle; not the rigid uptight image one normally associates with *Der Fuhrer*. And now that I have Hitler in my sights I just watch, remaining still, awaiting in stealth his next move.

The rally eventually ends and the crowd disperses in all directions. Young Adolph waltzes down a narrow cobblestoned road and descends into a beer cellar. I follow discreetly from behind and sidle up to a long wooden bar where a number of men, including Hitler, are lined up guzzling lager from large steins.

Put on the spot by the *barmann*, I point at the draft beer tap, and realize too late I have no native period currency to pay for it. Fortunately, the bartender is so busy he loses track of me.

Adolph downs the second half of his stein in one gulp while I'm still nursing mine. At first it looks like he's going to walk out, which means I'd have to sneak away without paying. But he abruptly changes direction, having apparently found what he is looking for—*Toilleten.*

I follow, my heart thumping wildly because this is my big chance to maybe be alone with Hitler and in a position to do the deed that needs to be done. I slip my right hand into my pocket and firmly clasp it around the folded dagger. Through the door, I glance around the men's room. Adolph is standing at a urinal, his back to me. No one else is present, not even in a toilet stall, and I know in my heart *it's now or never.* I pull The Godfather from my pocket and soft-shoe my way toward Hitler.

I freeze in my tracks.

Can't do it.

Adolph begins to zip up his trousers…

I regain my resolve and pounce, locking Hitler's midsection with my left arm, hugging him close, my breath on his neck, while with my right hand I flick the blade open and run its razor-sharp blade from the base of his left ear to his right.

Hitler struggles, blood spurting as if from a hose, confirming that I severed his carotid artery.

I jump back as Adolph slumps to the floor in a heap,

gurgling on his own blood, choking, bleeding out, a red pool widening beneath him.

As I clean my dagger on his lederhosen jacket, I can hardly believe I slit Hitler's throat—in a manner that would most certainly be lethal. I close the blade and return it to my pocket, then quickly rinse my hands and affect a hasty exit just as another man coming from the bar is about to enter.

I quicken my pace through the beer cellar and aim for the door and I hear the *barmann* shouting at me because I never paid for my beer, followed by more shouts emanating from *Toilleten*.

I discard my overcoat and hat and I launch, as fast as I've ever run my whole life, a mixture of fear and jubilation, adrenaline off the scales, endorphins shooting through my bloodstream.

I run and run and run until I reach a botanical garden, where I take refuge in a lush area of trees and shrubs.

Where's the exit photo?

Ah, just where it should be.

I remove the picture chosen by Chem from the envelope and study its image: a sweet-faced young female in a matching patterned short skirt and halter top standing on a calm waterfront somewhere, smiling at the camera. Behind her is a pier with a pavilion.

Cool. God bless Chem.

I would rather be anywhere than where I am right now, certain that my description has been provided to police by the bartender and they are already fanning out in search of the killer—me. But I would *especially* like to be in this "escape" image. Women may not understand it, thinking that their hair, or makeup, or perfume, is the key to attraction. But in reality, the best, easiest way for a woman to find a way into a man's heart is to simply… *smile.*

And so, I practically will myself into this photo, enjoying the suction that plants me standing directly in front of a truly gorgeous human being.

16.

"Hello," she mouths with her smiling lips, tingling my spine (in a good way), *nothing like Herr Boger.*

"Hi," I look up and down the quiet beach. The water is still, no waves, as if we are beside a lake, even if the breeze is salty.

"Where are we?"

"Why, Santa Monica," she says, still smiling.

"When?"

She chuckles. "Why, it's 1943, silly."

It seems so serene on this beach, more peaceful than the photograph does it justice.

I know I should focus on pulling myself out of here, back to Sausalito—the photo gallery—and my own time. But the magnetic attraction I have for this young woman is much stronger than the extraordinary pull I'd been feeling since getting drawn into images, what, five photographs ago?

"Would you like to walk along the tide with me?" she purrs.

And I realize there is nothing in this whole world—or wherever the hell (or heaven) I am—I'd like more at this moment (or any moment I can ever remember) than to walk the beach with this smiley young lady with the breathy voice.

She turns. "Let's go this way."

I don't need to be asked twice.

"Maybe we can get something to eat," she says. "A corn dog, maybe. Everyone's been talking about them, but I haven't had one yet and I hear they're very tasty."

Strolling by her side, I ask, "What do you do?"

"Me? I'm a senior at Van Nuys High. But not today," she laughs, and when this gal laughs, everything about the universe feels swell.

"Is it the weekend?" I ask.

"No, silly, it's a weekday. I'm skipping class." She pauses. "Again," she adds defiantly before glancing around. "Be on the lookout for truant officers." She freezes in her tracks and her smile disappears. "Uh-oh, you aren't one of those, are you?"

"One of what?"

"A truant officer."

"No, no."

"Because they're good at appearing out of nowhere."

I chuckle. "I've gotten good at appearing out of nowhere. But I'm not a truant officer."

"I know I'm behind the grind," she says, pouty-faced, so expressive she, "but I feel like a day at a beach." She resumes her stroll along with her million-dollar smile. "Don't you just feel like that sometimes?"

I realize that I should. A walk on the beach is good therapy for all that ails anyone.

A couple of men tossing a beach ball to one another whistle at her.

"Take no notice of the wolves," she says, blushing slightly, ignoring them, adding, "all the real men have gone to war."

I stop in my tracks. *She said 1943, didn't she?* "What war is that?"

"World War Two, silly," she says. "You sound like you're lost in a daydream. But that's okay. Daydreaming is my favorite thing to do in the whole world. I can daydream all day long."

Wait a friggin' second. My mind is racing. *Did I not put an end to Hitler?* And then I realize, there's always war, can't stop *that*. Must be some other tyrant acting out somewhere or other, or maybe it's Benito Mussolini, the Italian fascist, acting out all on his own—*would I have to find a photo of that arrogant bastard, too?*

"A penny for your thoughts," she says.

Snapping to, and hoping to put this matter to rest, I say, "I was thinking about… *Hitler*—heard of *him?*" I add quickly.

"A horrible, horrible man," she says, lips a-pout. "Hitler and his monstrous Nazis."

"Did you say *Nazis*?"

She squints at me, trying to understand, I guess, why, from her perspective, I'm so out of it. "What's your story, morning glory?"

I'd like to tell this glorious gal I just arrived here after *killing Hitler* except it would make no sense to her because, aside from anything else, I had very clearly *not* succeeded if Hitler was still alive. *But how could he survive a severed carotid artery?* I snap out of my thoughts once again and return my attention to this beautiful creature. "I'm just thinking how happy I am to make your acquaintance."

"You funny." She blushes. "Would you like to ride the carousel with me?" She doesn't wait for an answer but turns and strides off, calling back to me, "Shake a leg!"

I follow her, treading sand, and when I catch up she says, "I learn more things out of school than in."

"Like what?" I ask, amused.

"Like, breathing," she answers.

"What about breathing?" I indulge her.

"Would you eat through your nose?" she asks.

"I never have," I say.

"Exactly." She nods. "Because your nose is for breathing. But you'd be surprised how many people don't know that and breathe through their mouth."

"I've never really thought about," I say.

"I'm studying to be an actress," she says. "That's why I've learned how to breathe right. It's important. You know what the best thing to do is if you want to relax, like, you're about to do a scene and you're nervous and you need to calm down?"

I smile, so taken by her earnestness. "Please tell me."

"Take a deep breath," she says. "Like this."

I watch as she breathes slowly and deeply through her nose, holds the air in her lungs a beat, then exhales even more slowly through her mouth.

"Three times," she adds breathily, after the second. "Try it."

I stop and dig my feet into the sand, inhale deeply though my nose, wait a beat, and exhale super-slow through my mouth.

"Again," she says.

I follow her ritual, and wind up feeling even more relaxed than before.

"Well?"

"You're right!" I say, mildly tranquilized.

"You see?"

She giggles and reaches for my hand and we ascend a wooden staircase. As I step upon the pier a horn blares from a Series 90 Phaeton Oldsmobile, mint condition, swerving to avoid me before a colorful merry-go-round beckons us with its sheer beauty and elegance. A mercury dime from her change wallet produces a pair of tickets from the booth attendant and we climb aboard, astride two ornate horses, side by side. The carousel begins to circle, round and round, our wooden horses sliding up and down on gleaming brass poles to the accompaniment of organ music, with this young goddess gushing with glee.

She reaches for my hand, and hers feels so warm and soft and tingly in mine that I no longer care about Adolph Hitler and the war I tried to stop; I no longer care about anything except being here, in this moment of time, in this place, with this highly expressive, sensual and very passionate siren.

As the carousel picks up speed, I feel the kind of *whooshing* that normally accompanies the suctioning into vintage photographs, and I mentally fight it because I don't want to be yanked from this photo, at least not right now, maybe never.

She notices my disquiet and mouths *is something wrong* with lush lips as her horse rises and mine lowers—and I adore the way she does that, a powerful attraction she possesses almost as strong as the magnetic sideways gravity tugging at me without mercy.

I slide off the horse and assess angles for jumping from the platform, believing that if I can just stop the motion, maybe, just maybe, I'll be able to remain with her—here, in Santa Monica, in 1943.

She slides off her own horse and joins me at platform edge, and I realize, feeling the pull intensify, it's probably too late, I'm going.

"Hug me," I plead, a last-ditch effort, hoping maybe she can keep me anchored in space and time.

She wraps her arms around me and I hold her close, feeling the sweet scent of her breath against my face. I press my lips softly against her tender cheek.

"Deep breath," she whispers. "Breathe."

And then a power stronger than our union pries us apart, and I see this goddess shrinking smaller and smaller until she is just a speck, and then completely gone... and I find myself standing, once again, inside The Vintage Photo Gallery in Sausalito.

PART THREE

17.

"**N**o!" I cry in anguish.

"I know," says Chem, a look of deep concern on his face. "Hitler survived—and I know why."

"That's not what I'm talking about!"

"Then what?"

"I didn't want to leave that other photo you gave me!"

"What's that?" he says, snapping back from whatever he'd been dwelling on.

"I wanted to stay there!"

He shakes his head, chuckling. "I'm not surprised."

"Give it to me! That photo! I need to go straight back there right now!"

"To Hitler?"

"No! The other picture." I pause. "Wait a second, why did you say you're not surprised?"

"Because of *who* that person was."

"I don't care who she was—is—I just want to go back to her!"

"Didn't she tell you?"

"I never asked. It didn't matter!"

"Okay time-traveler, or photo-suck—I'm not sure what to call you—that young lady in the picture was—wait for it—Norma Jean!"

"Norma...?"

"Jean. As in, *Goodbye Norma Jean*," he sings. "*Though I never knew you at all.* The song? Elton John? Get it now?"

"You mean... you mean..." I am totally dumbfounded. "That was...*Marilyn Monroe?*"

"Duh." Chem puts a forefinger to his head. "That's exactly what I mean, man—but it was Marilyn *before* she became an actress and changed her name."

I find a chair and sit in it backwards, distraught, my head in my hands. I look up. "She had the most amazing smile!"

"I guess you just discovered why Marilyn broke so many hearts," he says. "And why her legacy endures. I once read that Joe DiMaggio never stopped loving her, even long after they divorced."

"And her voice! Oh-my-god, oh-my-god, oh-my-god." If I thought I'd lost my mind before, now I am sure of it, insanely in love with Marilyn Monroe, no, Norma Jean, no, someone in an image born long before me and already crossed over to the other side, and oh so tragically.

"Don't flip out on me, man!"

I look up, in deep despair. "Wasn't there a movie like this once?"

"Like what?"

"Where a guy goes back in time and falls in love?"

"Yeah, I remember," says Chem. "I think it was called Somewhere in Time. Set on Mackinac Island, on Lake Michigan. The male time traveler dies at the end."

"Gee, thanks for that." And then, more hopefully, I say, "Maybe I can go back into that picture and save Marilyn from herself. Or maybe from the Kennedy brothers."

"And do what? Marry her? Remain in that period the rest of your life and live happily ever after?" His eyes pop with incredulity. "Get a grip on yourself—you lovesick fool."

"Wait a minute." I look up at him. "Wait one friggin' minute. How did *you* know Hitler survived? I didn't even tell you what happened yet."

"Uh, I checked the names of those Nazi SS guys you met—Boger and Grabner?" Chem says sheepishly. "Both of them tried to flee—probably because of what you told them—but Maximilian Grabner got hanged in 1948 and Wilhelm Boger finally got arrested in 1958 and got convicted for murdering over a hundred people and died in prison."

"I am truly touched to hear that," I snap, "but don't change the subject on me. What about Adolph Hitler?"

"What about him?"

"I killed him!" I say. "I slit his throat. I cut his carotid artery. I watched him bleed out!

"Hey," he says, looking around. "What did you do with my coat and hat?"

"What coat and hat?"

"The coat and hat I gave you."

"Screw your coat and hat. I demand you answer me. How could Hitler have possibly survived having his throat cut?"

Chem is unnaturally silent. "Because," he finally says, "Hitler wasn't there."

"What do you mean he wasn't there? You told me he was there, in Munich, in the photo—and I *saw* him there!"

"He wasn't in the original photograph," says Chem. "It was just a hoax."

"What the hell are you talking about, just a hoax?"

"I did some research while you were away." Chem grabs a chair and sits himself next to me, looking down, twiddling his thumbs. "Hitler's image was in the photograph

I showed you, that's true. But he was never really there in real life—that is, where and when the picture was taken. It turns out that in 1928 Heinrich Hoffman doctored his own photograph. He *added* Adolph to the image to make it *look* as if Hitler was in the crowd."

"Why the hell would he do that?" I holler in frustration.

"Hitler wanted himself inserted into the photo for use in Nazi propaganda. It took decades to prove it was a fake. But it's proven. Hitler wasn't there that day."

"Yes, he was there! I saw him! I *killed* him!"

Chem shakes his head. "You *thought* you saw him there because he was in the photograph, which is where you were, inside a photo. But you didn't kill Hitler; you *couldn't* have killed Hitler, because he *wasn't there*. You killed a *phantom*."

"I killed a what?"

"A phantom."

"You damn old fool!" I get off the chair and kick it away. "Of all the photos you might have given me of Hitler before he was famous, you give me the one where he's an *add-on*? A phantom? Sonofabitch!"

He shrugs, all innocence. "Don't go postal on me, man. I didn't know until *after* you went into the photo that it was a fraud."

"Oh, that's real cute. And then you get me all lovesick over Marilyn Monroe! THIS WHOLE THING IS NUTS!"

The old hippie shrugs. "I told you to put your sanity aside."

"Goddammit! Why does everybody keep telling me that?"

Chem puts his hands up in surrender mode. "Hey man, you're freaking out."

"Freaking out? I've just played pool with Mark Twain, stopped JFK from getting assassinated, almost got tortured in Auschwitz, *murdered* someone—Hitler—in cold blood, cut his throat using my own hands, and then met Marilyn Monroe while she was still a teenager, and rode on a carousel with her—and then got separated from my soulmate just as we were starting to hug and kiss and fall in love. Why *shouldn't* I be freaking out?"

He leans forward. "You didn't ball her, did you?"

"What? None of your business you crazy old hippie! If you must know, I had a *spiritual* connection with her! Did anyone ever tell you that you have putrid breath in addition to a dirty mind?"

"Is it?"

"You kidding? It's like you've been puking all day. Now listen to me, I need more pictures of Norma Jean, and I need them pronto—where's your *Famous Actress* category?"

"You're deluding yourself," says Chem. "This can't end well."

"Whatever," I call back.

Down the aisle I discover a shelf labeled *Entertainers Women* and I riffle through assorted photos, each labeled with their names: Katherine Hepburn, Elizabeth Taylor, Lauren Bacall, Louise Brooks, Grace Kelly… *wait a second.* I flip backwards. "What the…?" I wonder aloud.

"What is it?" queries Chem, peering over my shoulder. "That's not Marilyn."

"No, it sure isn't," I say. "I know it sounds crazy but *this* is the woman I met on the plane!"

"What plane?"

"I told you already: The plane that brought me here from Santa Barbara—the last flight out. Who is she?"

"Is? I think you mean *was*." Chem shakes his head, gazing upon the photograph. "*Very* past tense, dude. Louise Brooks was a dancer, a flapper girl—and then a silent film star. Some call her the 'lost star' of the 1920s. When she died a few decades ago, Louise Brooks was a lot older than she is in this photograph, so I very much doubt…"

"She was on my plane, sitting across the aisle from me, and we had a long chat."

"Maybe it was someone who *looked* like her," he says.

"No," I say, incredulous, studying the image. "It was definitely the woman in this picture. Same exact hairstyle…"

"Yep," Chem nods. "Lulu was famous for creating the bob. She made it trendy in her time."

"Yes. Lulu. That was Louise's nickname. Louise, Lulu— get it? And her character in *Pandora's Box*, her best known movie, was named Lulu."

I'm shaking my head. "*Lulu* was the name of the woman I met on the plane. She had the exact same eyes, nose, lips and teeth. It was… it had to be… Louise Brooks."

"But how could that be possible—unless it was her ghost?"

"You're asking *me?* I don't know how *any of this* is possible! Come to think of it, when we first started talking I noticed that she looked like she was from another time, the things she wore, the way she expressed herself, the way she spoke, and especially the way she wore her hair."

"Lulu was written about as a magical presence," says Chem.

"Why does that not surprise me?" I say. "She's the reason I came to Sausalito."

"How's that?" Chem cups a hand over his left ear.

"She suggested I come here after I told her I had no idea where I was going next. *And* she recommended *this* photo gallery."

The old hippie considers this with a grin. "That's very ironic," he says, nodding.

"Dare I ask, why?"

"Because Lulu lived the last thirty years of her life in Rochester, New York."

I throw up my arms in exasperation. "So?"

"You don't know?" Chem shakes his head, his saggy face splashed with disdain. "Rochester is *huge* for a photo buff like me. Ever heard of Eastman-Kodak? Rochester was where the *Kodak Moment* got born. And the old Eastman

House has the most important photography museum in the world. Louise Brooks moved there just so she could be near the museum because that's where they keep all her old films. This is blowing my mind."

"*Your* mind? What the hell is going on with this gallery of yours?"

"This gallery of *mine?* What's going on here is more about *your* mind than *my* gallery."

"Look, here's something *real* that came from Lulu." I reach down into my shirt.

"What is it?"

I hold out the silver pendant. "She called it a Coptic Cross, from Ethiopia. She was wearing it. And then she put it around my neck and insisted I keep it."

Chem inspects the cross. "Hmm. Talismans like this can be very powerful."

"You think I'm nuts?"

"I can't say. But I know just the person who might know."

"Then get him on the phone," I say, "because this is freaking me out even worse than before."

Chem points to another aisle of photographs.

"You mean?"

"I do. Another portrait." He saunters off and returns a minute later with a sepia-toned photo of a stern-looking gentleman in a three-piece woolen suit, late 1930s by the look of him.

"Sigmund Freud?" I guess.

Chem nods. "Why not let the master decide?"

"This isn't about psychiatry," I say, somewhat offended. "This is about physics. Do you have a photo of Albert Einstein? Maybe this fits into his theory of relativity. Wasn't that somehow connected to the speed of light and time travel?"

"This isn't about physics," says the old hippie. "This is about *meta*physics."

"Works for me."

He slaps his forehead. "I don't have a new age section. Too new."

"What about…?"

"Shh!" he shushes me. "I'm thinking." He closes his eyes and twirls his forefinger near the side of his head. "Eureka!"

"Eureka? I never thought anyone actually said that outside of comic books."

He winks. "Maybe that's because you haven't been to Humboldt County. My grass farm up near Eureka is what keeps this place in clover."

I should have known.

He bounds off to *Literary Figures* and returns with a photo of…

Kurt Vonnegut, Jr.

"Vonnegut? Why Vonnegut?"

"You kidding me?" says the old hippie. "Vonnegut is the master at this kind of thing!"

"How so?"

"Did you *never* read Slaughterhouse Five? In its very first line Vonnegut's protagonist, Billy Pilgrim, comes *unstuck in time*. Just like you. You are unstuck in time. Vonnegut will be able to make sense of this better than anyone because he *invented* this sort of thing."

"Will he be able to introduce me to Marilyn Monroe?"

Chem arches an eyebrow. "You really are smitten, aren't you? Looks to me that even if Vonnegut ever knew Marilyn it wouldn't matter because this particular photo was snapped long after she died. But that's a good thing."

"Why a good a thing?"

"Because Kurt will be all the wiser as an older man."

I study the picture: Vonnegut, shock of thick hair, trademark moustache, perched upon a bench in a park somewhere. "I suppose it's worth a..."

18.

Before I can finish my sentence, I'm sitting on a bench facing Kurt Vonnegut, Jr. His eyes are tired and fuzzy and he is looking straight at me with a mildly amused if unfazed expression by my sudden appearance.

Finally, he speaks, and his mid-Western twang and general demeanor reminds me of his literary hero Mark Twain. "Are you on an adventure?"

I feel reassured. "How did you know?"

"Well, you just appeared on a bench next to me completely out of nowhere," he drawls. "So, either *you* are on an adventure, or *I* have been drinking too much."

"I'm unstuck in time," I blurt, "just like Billy Pilgrim, the protagonist in your sci-fi book."

"It's *mainstream*," growls Vonnegut, somewhat irritated, "*not* sci-fi."

"Okay, okay, sorry about that. *Mainstream*. But in my case, I travel back and forth in time by getting pulled into old photographs and popped out again—and sometimes from photo to photo."

He coughs, a smoker's hack. "I am very familiar with how that works." He checks and rechecks all of his pockets looking for something and comes up empty. "You wouldn't happen to have a Pall Mall, would you?"

"No, sorry. Do you know why I can travel in photographs?"

"Of course."

"Will you tell me?"

He hesitates. "You won't like the answer," he says.

"But I should probably know it anyway, given my situation, no?"

He shrugs. "I'm not sure how much good it will do you."

"But I'd like to know. I feel like I've gone temporarily insane."

"Could be the other way around," says Vonnegut.

"How so?"

"Maybe you are temporarily sane." He pauses. "Here's the deal: If you fetch me a pack of Pall Malls and matches, I'll explain it to you."

"Where?"

Vonnegut points over my shoulder. "City Smoke Shop, Second Avenue and Forty-Sixth Street."

"Where are we?"

"Dag Hammarskjold Plaza, near the UN building."

"New York City?"

Vonnegut nods.

"Okay, I'll be right back."

I get up and race out of the Plaza onto Second Avenue amid drivers blaring their car horns. I quickly find City Smoke Shop, stand impatiently behind someone gabbing about one cigar or another, buy a pack of Pall Malls, grab a box of matches, and race back.

Vonnegut is gone!

"Shit, shit, shit!" I shout, looking all around frantically.

I notice a bag lady sitting on a bench feeding pigeons. "Where'd he go?" I holler at her.

She points the same direction where Vonnegut pointed me.

"Sonofabitch!" I hustle back toward Second Avenue and

look up and down the long boulevard, traffic continuing to produce a discordant mixture of notes.

"What time is it?" I bark at a hot dog vendor on the corner.

"Lunchtime," he barks back. "Wanna dog?"

"No. Did you happen to see an older man with a full head of hair and a bristly moustache come by?"

"Every day." The vendor smirks.

"Where'd he go?"

"Wanna dog?" he asks.

"Okay, okay—give me a dog."

Only after we've exchanged a dog for cash does he point to the corner of East Fiftieth Street.

I bound across the road and almost get run over twice in the process, drivers cursing at me. I drop the hot dog dripping with mustard and relish into a trash bin and enter an Italian restaurant called Lasagna.

And there he is, Kurt Vonnegut, Jr. sitting with his back to the wall, a fork in his hand, picking on a Caesar salad. Diners at other tables are smoking cigarettes, the air a haze of second-hand nicotine—was life really like this not that long ago?

I approach gingerly. Vonnegut looks up from his salad and waves me away with both hands.

"But I have your cigarettes."

I hold out the pack of Pall Malls.

"Oh, it's you." He gestures to the chair opposite him. "You might as well sit."

I plunk myself down.

"Matches?" he says.

I hand him the box of matches, too. "I didn't know where you went," I say.

"If you found me at Dag Hammarskjold Plaza, I figured you could find me anywhere. I'm hungry. And this is where I eat every day."

The server swaps out Vonnegut's empty salad dish with a bowl of linguine and clam sauce. Kurt savors the garlicky aroma and looks up at me. "So, what can I do for you?"

"You said you knew about how I'm able to travel back in time through photographs and you said you'd tell me if I fetched you a pack of Pall Malls," I say in one burst of a breath, pointing to the cigarettes.

"Ah, yes," he twangs. Using a spoon, Italian-style, Vonnegut coils linguine around his fork, brings it to his mouth and chews slowly, relishing its flavor as if the very moment depended on it. Then he plants his eyes directly into mine.

"Are you certain," he asks softly, "that you really want to know?"

My heart is thumping as I sit with my eardrums riveted

to his every word. "Yes, I'm sure. *Very* sure. Please, I *need* to know."

"Okay, but don't say I didn't warn you." He takes another bite of pasta, enjoys it just as rapturously and deliberately as the bite before. "It's actually very simple."

"Simple is good," I nod approvingly, sitting on the edge of my chair in anticipation.

Vonnegut pauses to sip iced tea (or maybe Dewar's) and looks me straight in the eye. "It's all an illusion."

"A what?"

"Just like Billy Pilgrim, you are…"

I expect Vonnegut to say *unstuck in time*.

But he does not.

Vonnegut says, "Just like Bill Pilgrim… *you are a character in a book.*"

I recoil in horror. "Huh?"

"You're not real." He puts down his spoon and fork, leans back and smiles smugly. "You're just a fictional character that some author is writing about."

"That's ridiculous." I cross my arms indignantly.

"I told you that you wouldn't like it."

"But what about you?"

"Me?" Vonnegut points at himself with his thumb. "I'm dead."

"Then what are you doing *here?* How am I *looking* at you?"

"Trying to enjoy lunch? Dealing with your existential drama? I actually don't know, except that I used to like this place—and Dag Hammarskjold Plaza—a pleasant spot from which to watch life go by in a world gone mad."

"You're saying you're a ghost?"

"I guess to you I am an apparition, a specter, something you've made up in your mind, perhaps with the help of a photograph, maybe coupled with the soul that got freed from my decrepit old body when I crossed over." He sighs. "There's no time like the past. But—past, present or future—it all really depends on what the *author* is thinking. The author is in control of this scenario, not you. Believing otherwise is a young man's fancy." I guess Vonnegut can tell by my expression that I am somewhat discombobulated by his nutty news. Because he adds, "There's no point worrying about it. It's not like you can *do* anything about it. We are *all* characters of someone else's making."

"So…so… so if I'm just a character in a book and you're dead, what are we doing here?"

"Here? As in existence?"

"Yes. Existence. This place. Both, I guess."

"Suchness and that-ness," he says. "I guess you could say we are trapped in the amber of the moment. Beyond that, it's all a lie." He pauses. "You hear that?" He cocks his ear upward to the strains of Louis Armstrong singing, *I see trees of green, red roses too, I see them bloom for me and you. And I think to myself what a wonderful world.* "Music is proof of the existence of God. It is so extraordinarily full of magic."

With that, Vonnegut tosses some cash on the table, un-crumples himself from his chair and strolls off, leaving the linguine mostly uneaten, and I'm left sitting by myself, dumbfounded, thinking, *I'm no better off than before*; worse, actually. Out of the picture. Literally. *And what now?*

I look around the restaurant for photographs to escape into but none grace its walls. So instead I wander out onto Second Avenue, back to Dag Hammarskjold Plaza, try to find the pair of benches where Vonnegut and I had been sitting. But I hadn't been paying attention earlier and I discover there are too many benches from which to choose.

So, somewhat disoriented, I seat myself upon a random bench. And I sit and I sit and I sit, as mid-afternoon sunshine turns to dusk, and dusk eventually to dark, willing a breeze, anything, to whoosh me back to Sausalito.

That's it, I say, resigned to my fate. I've gone too far and now I'm stuck, in New York City, a decade earlier than from where and when I'm supposed to be. I give up—a surrender to my predicament—and after hours of sitting and waiting for a metaphysical suction that does not come, I rise from the bench and forlornly set off on a walk across town, turn left on Lexington Avenue, cross Forty-Second street, and keep going all the way down to Gramercy Park. I stroll around this gated, private square, cut down Irving Place and, passing a tavern, the thought occurs to me that a Bombay Sapphire martini may be just what I need, for body and soul—*it certainly can't hurt!* So, I enter the shabby saloon favored, apparently, by O. Henry, stool myself at the bar and order one just the way I like it, leave the shaker.

Glancing around, this way and that, I notice that the themed décor of this bar is… vintage photograph.

So, I know deep inside that I'm finally on the right track, in the right place, with the right libation before me. But it is also important to shield my eyes and ensure I don't get pulled into *any* old picture, but one of my own choosing.

As the bartender serves my cocktail, I say, with as much nonchalance as I can muster, "Cool pics on the wall. Do you happen to have any of…?" I gulp. "…Of Marilyn Monroe?"

"Oh yeah," he says. "We've got that famous flying skirt photo."

"Which is that?"

"The one where Marilyn is standing on a subway grate

on Lexington Avenue, a whooshing of air from a train passing below lifts her skirt and she's fighting to cover up her panties. See for yourself."

"Where?" I ask.

"Down there," he points behind me.

"Thanks," I say, not turning around, not taking any chances with the other images. "I look forward to checking it out."

Slowly, I sip my martini, allowing its warm tingling to slip down my gullet and spread throughout my body, relaxing my mind.

No need to hurry, take it slow, I'll soon be with the woman of my dreams again.

Only when I finally drain the martini am I ready.

"Another libation?" asks the bartender.

I answer his question with one of my own. "How far down the wall is that photo of Marilyn Monroe?"

He looks up and squints over my shoulder.

"About twenty feet, I guess."

"Thank you."

I de-stool and set off, averting my eyes from the long row of photos I discern through peripheral vision. Only when I've walked twenty feet do I turn to face Marilyn.

Except that's not what I immediately see.

Because Marilyn is not directly in front of me.

No, she is *beside* the picture I'm now looking at—in abject horror, I might add.

Because after a moment's whooshing I find myself facing Leatherface—the inbred maniacal murderer from *The Texas Chainsaw Massacre.*

And he's trotting straight at me with his chainsaw!

19.

I can feel Leatherface gaining ground from behind. The thunderous buzzing of his chainsaw fills my ears with all its ghastliness, a smell of blood and death in my nostrils, and my heart is pounding.

Never in my life, not even in Auschwitz, have I felt so panic-stricken as I do right now.

I trip on a rock, fall to the ground and Leatherface is upon me, towering over my prostrate form, slobbering beneath his mask of human skin, poised to strike at any moment, chainsaw raised over his head.

I do as Marilyn instructed, a deep breath through my nose, hold a beat, and exhale slowly through my mouth.

"So," Leatherface growls into my face. "How do you like Texas in summer?"

I don't answer, cannot speak.

He lowers the chainsaw in slow motion, stopping every few inches to extract as much fright from my eyes

as possible. Lower, lower, his buzzing, bloodied blade is moving ever closer to my face.

I take another two deep breaths.

"Lick my plate," Leatherface adds.

The vibration of the chainsaw, now only inches from my nose, combined with my deep breathing, causes a sucking sensation, which turns into a *whooshing,* and…

20.

"**S**nap out of it!" says Chem, inside the Vintage Photo Gallery, his eyes wide and fixated upon me. "Are you okay?"

Coming out of it, I hear Jim Morrison crooning through crackly speakers, *Let's swim to the moon...*

I look up, down and all around. "Am I okay?" I holler feverishly. "No, I am not okay! That maniac in The Texas Chainsaw Massacre was about a nano-second away from slicing and dicing my head into barbeque and chili!"

"Bummer," says Chem.

"You and your friggin *bummer*! You have no friggin' idea!" I grab a paper towel from his desk and dab my face, soaking up perspiration.

"What about Vonnegut?" he asks.

"What about him?"

"Did you see him, too?"

"Of course," I say, still trembling, looking around

for something to sit on and regain my composure, pull myself together.

"What did he say?"

"Hold on." I sit upon a low stool and take a deep breath—three—just like Marilyn taught me. "He said he was dead."

"Dead?"

"That's right, dead. Which implies I'm seeing ghosts when I travel to the past through photographs."

Chem shakes his head. "He was just messing with your head, man. Time travel and ghosts are two different things."

"Ah, you're suddenly an expert?"

Chem sticks to his clinician pose. "Didn't he have anything else to say?"

"Yes, he did."

"What?"

"Vonnegut told me I'm just a character in a book."

Chem takes a long moment to consider this. "Of course, he would. He's a writer, so that's how he thinks. He creates characters and plots. He creates whole little worlds called *books*. Vonnegut is God to his characters. He's saying we are *all* characters to a larger God."

"But what if he's right?"

"Which part?"

"That I'm just a character in a book—and you are, too, by extension?"

"What? He was talking to *you*, man, not *me*. I know *I'm* real."

"How do you know for sure?"

He holds up a reefer, takes a hit and blows it out. "I smoke therefore I am. What you're saying is crazy."

"Oh, really. Wouldn't you say getting pulled into old photos is crazy?"

"Yes, except if I heard you correctly from a few photos ago, you prevented the assassination of President John Kennedy." He squints at me. "Is that really for real?"

I digest this, unsure of anything, other than that Chem is more stoned than usual. "I'm not sure what's real anymore and what isn't. I think I just need to go home and get my head straight."

"I get that, man. You sound fried to me."

"And you're not?"

Chem closes one eye and looks at me with the other. "Didn't you say one of the pictures you saw here looked like someone you met on the airplane you flew on to get here?"

"Not *looked like*. It *was* her—Louise Brooks."

"That's right, Lulu. And you said she's the person who recommended Sausalito to you?"

"*And* this shop."

"So that means she's it, man."

"It?"

"The portal. You need to talk to Lulu." He trots off, grabs a photo, and trots back, his beaded necklace dancing around his neck. "Here you go."

"Wait a minute," I say. "That's not Louise Brooks... That's..."

"Changed my mind, this will be better than Lulu. It's Rod..."

21.

Before Chem can finish his sentence, I'm looking directly into the grim countenance and piercing dark brown eyes of Rod Serling, creator of the highly acclaimed 1960s television series *The Twilight Zone*.

Serling is standing in front of a wire link fence with a large sign that says *Terminal* pointing to my right. His hair is jet black and he is slimmer, and shorter (about five-five), than I might have otherwise imagined.

"Got a match?" he asks, removing a cigarette from a pack of Viceroys.

"Sorry, no." And I'm thinking, jeez, *everyone* smoked.

"Never mind." He searches the pockets of his black suit jacket and locates a small matchbox—black and orange— from The Brown Derby, a once renowned but long-gone Hollywood restaurant.

"Am I…" I break his silence. "Am I… am I… in… *The Twilight Zone*?"

Rod Serling shakes his head, and his face is neither grim nor smiley but matter-of-fact, and he speaks with a steady crisp voice. "You're not in any episode *I* ever produced in five seasons on the air."

"Then where?"

He takes a long draw from his cigarette. "What if I said, Welcome to the world of quantum entanglement?"

This stumps me. "Quantum... what?"

"Traveling from photograph to photograph, going back in time, trying to change history, and actually *succeeding*." He grins, as if he is mildly impressed. "What would *you* call it?"

"I'm not sure. Absurd?"

Serling nods. "The *whole world* is absurd." He takes

another puff, blows smoke rings, seemingly in deep thought. "And it is also mysterious. Albert Einstein called quantum entanglement *spooky action at a distance.*"

"Meaning?"

"It means that two entangled particles separated by long distances can instantly affect each other."

"I'm not getting it," I say. "Almost all of this is way over my head."

"It suggests," says Serling, "that Einstein was right when he said, and I quote, 'The distinction between the past, present and future is only an illusion, however persistent.'" He smiles. "I'm not sure I could have written what's happening to you any better myself." He pauses. "Though it most certainly lies between science and superstition, my old specialty."

"I am truly complimented," I say. "But I'd actually like to *reverse* what's going on with me and return to my normal reality. Is that possible?"

Rod considers my words. "I can approach this only from the standpoint of how it would turn out if it were *me* writing this story," he says, reminding me of Vonnegut's words about an author being in control.

He inhales deeply from his cigarette before blowing smoke toward the heavens, which he studies, for inspiration, perhaps.

"Please feel welcome to take a stab," I say, having confidence in the ability of the grand master of magic realism to grasp a situation such as mine—and maybe even turn this sucker around.

"If this were my story," he finally says, stroking his chin, still looking up to the sky, "the reader would eventually discover that you are the unwitting subject of a quantum entanglement experiment being conducted on a sound stage by scientists in the U.S. military-industrial establishment."

He pauses to ponder on. "Or maybe you have inadvertently penetrated a parallel dimension of some kind." Then he returns his gaze upon me. "Or maybe you were trying so hard to escape your normal existence, your normal thinking patterns, that you brought quantum entanglement upon yourself." He nods. "Yes, I think I like that one best. But whichever it is," he adds, "you've been given a special gift, being able to cross like this into the photon clock."

"The what?"

"It's complicated," says Serling. He takes another long drag from his cigarette. "And I don't really have a horse to run in this race. I'm only here because I got invoked somehow, a spirit that has a body again—maybe you had been thinking of me?"

I shrug. And I do remember, though I keep this

thought to myself, that the sky where I'd parked near Santa Barbara airport had indeed reminded me of *The Twilight Zone* intro.

"Do you know how young I was when I died?" asks Rod.

"I think I recall you died way before your time."

Serling nods. "I chain-smoked these coffin nails." He holds his cigarette out and studies the smoke curling upward into the air. "Four packs a day. Every day. And I worked myself to an early death at the age of fifty. Open-heart surgery nailed me. But I knew when I was getting rolled into the operating room that my odds had been better surviving World War Two, where I not only saw action in the Philippines but nearly got myself killed. And I carried those terrible experiences with me the rest of my life. Literally. I still have shrapnel in one wrist and one of my knees. Sometimes, going down stairs, my knee just gives out and I fall flat on my face." He drags another dose of nicotine. "You know what I do about it?"

I shake my head.

Rod looks me straight in the eye. "I get back up again." He pauses. "Do *you* walk around every day with physical pain?"

"No."

"Have you ever been to war?"

"No."

With his free hand, Serling points to his head. "Let me tell you, the emotional scars from battle are worse than physical wounds. I know because I suffered both. The mental wound is a different kind of scar but more profound—an ache we carry that no medic can ever cure. I call it *mind pain*. When my father died, I was still overseas and, though the war had already ended, they wouldn't give me emergency leave to attend his funeral." He falters, choking back emotion. "I always wear this." He pulls up his sleeve to display a paratrooper bracelet on his right wrist. "I wear it in memory of my father. You know why?"

I shake my head.

"Because I've always believed my dad made a deal with a higher power to sacrifice his life for mine. So that I would come home alive from World War Two."

He pauses to compose himself. "That's right, I think he exchanged his life for mine. Absurd, huh? I wrote a *Twilight Zone* episode about it. *In Praise of Pip.*" He pauses. "War and killing is a devastating experience for people. You should feel very grateful for not having had to endure any of that, and not having to carry it with you every day the rest of your life. And every night. The nightmares..." he trails off.

"The only reason I turned to writing, Rod continues, "was to try to get it all off my chest. And what happens? I end up living in Bubble land."

"Bubble land?"

"Hollywood's a great place to live… if you're a grapefruit. Mink coats and swimming pools—and whenever someone serves you a glass of water it comes with a huge dollop of whipped cream."

He pauses. "And what do I get for my huge success?"

I cock my head.

"Ulcers." He grimaces and takes another deep hit from his cigarette. "Fighting the networks over commercial sponsors. It's tough, you know, to produce incisive social commentary when every twelve minutes you're interrupted by twelve dancing rabbits singing about toilet paper."

He pauses and looks me straight in the eye. "You know, you should feel very grateful to be alive, to be living without the physical and emotional wounds of war. We never know where or when our physical body will give up the soul. But you know what was, for me, the predominant fear when, a day before my operation, I realized I might die on the operating table, as I soon did?"

I shake my head.

"The relationships that would end." He takes a final puff of his cigarette and drops it to the ground, stomps it out, and immediately lights up another. "After we're gone," he continues, "evidence of our once physical being can be found only in photographs. And maybe what you've encountered is an essence of our souls that continues to reside in those impressions." He pauses to consider his words. "The Indians had a perspective on that."

"You mean Native Americans?"

Serling smirks. "I may be the least prejudiced person you'll ever meet—and that was reflected in all of the *Zone* episodes I wrote myself. But in my time, we called them Indians. And Indians called the camera a *spirit box*. You see, the Indians truly believed that the camera would capture their spirit and that they would lose part of their soul to their appearance in a photograph. Truth is, behind us we leave traces—remnants, molecules—of what we once were. We leave them in all kinds of places, including the photographs that recorded our once physical presence. Call it a frozen moment in time. In your case, you appear to have fallen under the spell of gelatin emulsion and silver halide crystals."

He takes yet another long drag from his cigarette. "This is about Quantum entanglement, the photon clock, and even that fifth dimension I felt compelled to write about after returning home from the war, as a means of expressing moralism and social justice."

He pauses. "Come to think of it, before Twilight Zone

I wrote a teleplay called The Time Element. It incorporated time travel, but not photographs. In my story, it is 1958—the year it was broadcast—and the protagonist has a reoccurring dream about being in Pearl Harbor on December sixth, 1941, one day before the Japanese pulled their sneak attack. In his dream, he tries to warn everyone about what is about to happen, but nobody listens. He's telling all this to a psychiatrist in 1958. But when the psychiatrist looks up from his notes the patient is no longer there. The shrink goes to a bar, orders a drink, sees a photo of his patient on the wall and asks the bartender about him. That's when he learns that the patient died seventeen years earlier at Pearl Harbor."

"Imaginative," I say.

"Thank you. The success of that show—a one-off—led to CBS pulling the Zone out of mothballs and into production."

He pauses. "There is still so much we don't understand." He flicks his left wrist to check the time on his triangular Hamilton Ventura wristwatch, turns around to look at the sign—Terminal—above him, and looks back at me. "Ah," he says, grinning.

"What time is it?" I ask.

"Now," he replies. "Now it is time for you to visit The Terminal."

"Where?" I ask. "I don't see any terminal."

"Just follow the arrow." He stretches his arm to point at the sign. "It's about a hundred yards over the rim." He smiles and pulls another long drag from his cigarette. "And put your sanity aside."

22.

I'm looking ahead of me. *Rim? What rim?*

But I nonetheless walk along the wire link fence for about a hundred yards and, not seeing any terminal, or anything at all, I look back to Rod Serling. But he is no longer there.

However, when I turn around again I am amazed to see that I'm standing smack in front of a large building: The Terminal.

Sliding doors automatically open and I enter. The building is high-ceilinged and cavernous, like an old airline terminal, illuminated with harsh fluorescent tube lighting. Primitive check-in desks line the back wall, but the terminal is otherwise eerily sparse and quiet with no sign of life—*where is everybody?*

"Hello?" I call out.

My own voice echoes back at me. *Hello, Hello, Hellooooo?*

At the far end of The Terminal, a door cracks open,

widens, and an oddly familiar person walks out and begins bounding toward me.

As he comes nearer, I discern who this is, leaving me totally and utterly astonished.

He waves and calls out cheerfully. "Hello!"

Hello! Hello! Hellooooo!

I remain still, frozen in my tracks, mesmerized by what I see, and leaving me in no doubt whatsoever that I have truly put all sanity aside.

While I had no idea what or whom Rod Serling sent me to encounter, other than it would likely be absurd, the very last person I expected to meet was…

Myself.

Me, or the apparition, with the same kind of posture and body language as mine, continues striding briskly over to where I'm stuck in place. He is smiling, my smile, and offers his hand, identical to mine, and by reflex I grip and shake it, an exact match.

"Are you… are you… *me?*" I ask.

He shakes his head, beaming. "Of course not."

"Then… *who?*"

"I was your identical twin."

"What?"

"I was there with you in our mother's womb—but only at the very beginning of our conception. I did not survive. Not as a physical being, anyway. But we all move on as spirits, whether delivered or not."

I say, "But I didn't have an identical twin."

"Yes." He winks. "You did. Me. But nobody ever knew, not even our parents or the obstetrician."

"How is that possible?"

"You went one way, and I another. We fought," he adds, shrugging. "You won."

"I killed you?"

He nods, still grinning. "You were too young to know what you were doing, and so was I. We were fighting over nutrients from our mother."

"How does that work?" I ask.

"The actual name for it is Vanishing Twin Syndrome. Your fetus absorbed mine, the fetus that I was, physically."

"Oh my God, that's terrible!" I say

"Don't let it bother you." He continues to smile, almost whimsically. "It is not only normal but happens more often than most people know."

"So, what are you doing *here?*" I ask, awed by this revelation.

"Meeting *you*, of course. It is an extremely rare opportunity and I am very delighted to be here. I've tried before."

"You have?"

"Yes, in your dreams at night. Twice. But you did not awaken to it."

I am speechless, not knowing what else to say.

He chuckles.

"It must seem bizarre to you," he said. "But there are so many things those delivered into the world do not understand. Not until they cross over."

"Are you here to tell me about such things?"

"No." He shakes his head. "I'm not allowed."

"Why not?"

"Life is *supposed* to be mysterious where you are. The best thing you can do is to surrender to the mystery and enjoy the wonderment of it all. I'm here to convey that you were given a gift I was not, and that you're not doing your best to enjoy it."

I cock my head. "What do you mean?"

"You were given the gift of this life, a transition from the *before* to the *after*. Life is designed to be challenging, full of complexities, full of stresses."

I nod. It is as if this thing, a twin, a doppelganger, or truly another *me*, knows my innermost thoughts. The only difference is that he is smiling and I am not, and I'm standing here trying to discern which is the more fortunate, happier soul.

"You can live burdened by whatever is bothering you,"

he continues. "Or you can see each day as an opportunity to smile, be happy, and experience something new."

He pauses. "There is nothing wrong with escapism once in a while. But you have to face your own reality. Embrace it. And the best way to do that is to invest your thoughts wisely. As you think, you shall be. You have the power to take control of your mind, lose the clutter, and resurrect the world around you. Would you like to know the secret to happiness?"

I nod.

"Not minding what happens, whatever it is that's happening, just flow with it. Flow like water, the essence of life, and never get stuck. Because all you truly own is the moment."

"A few fleeting seconds?"

"One way to look at this is by turning time, in your mind, into an ever-present moment." He studies my eyes, watching me struggle with this concept.

"Another way to live your life in the present, if ever you begin to worry about anything, is to tell yourself that between now and bedtime is all that matters."

He pauses. "May I add something to that?"

"Please."

"Meaning and magic is all around you, all the time. All you need to do is open your soul to it." He pauses.

"May I also tell you what I've learned from spirits who once lived long productive lives and now reside where I do?"

"Yes."

"I learned about their biggest regrets. It is so sad that they should have regrets—don't you think?"

"I do."

"Most of them say they did not try hard enough to fulfill their dreams. And they say that they did not spend more time with their kids and companions, or that they did not express their true feelings as much as they might have. Or that they did not stay in touch with friends."

He pauses. "Are you getting all this?"

"I am."

"But most of all, they say they didn't laugh as much as they might have. Or forgive enough." He stops to focus his eyes directly into mine. "You don't really want to leave the amusement park without taking the roller-coaster, do you?"

"I guess not."

"Don't leave your present embodiment into your soul's next phase with regrets or hatred in your heart for anything or anyone. Don't fret about the future or ruminate the past, or ever take yourself too seriously. Instead, savor every moment with whimsy, and always focus on one thing at a time, maximize your senses. If you take care of the moment, the days, weeks and months fall into place and take care of themselves. Oh, and pay attention to your dreams." He offers an envelope to me. "Please take this."

"What is it?" I ask with no small amount of trepidation.

"A photograph."

But of course.

I look down at the envelope, intrigued but unsure whether to look inside, and also a tad sorry if this is meant to conclude our extraordinary exchange.

"Are you certain?" I say.

He nods, smiling. "I'm certain you would be lost forever without it."

I accept the envelope.

He turns to leave and looks back at me. "Oh, and..."

"Put my sanity aside?"

He nods, grinning. "Yes. But also, this: awaken."

"Will I ever see you again?" I whisper.

He does not answer, and I ask again, louder. But he just continues walking until he reaches the portal he'd walked through at the far end of The Terminal—and disappears from my sight.

I open the envelope and find a photograph: the cockpit of a vintage airplane...

23.

No sooner do I look at this photograph than I am part of it, inside the cockpit, and a loud rattling fills my ears from a pair of spinning propellers, engines revving, on a runway poised for imminent departure.

I look left, out of the window and see the wings, and I discern this handsome aircraft to be a Douglas DC-3 from the 1930s, albeit in pristine condition.

A voice crackles through an old speaker in the cockpit. "Last Flight Out cleared for takeoff."

Suddenly, the plane lurches forward even though there is no pilot and no co-pilot in the two seats facing the instrument panel.

"Wait!" I call out to whomever is instructing me. "There's no one here to fly the plane!"

"Yes," the voice returns. "*You* are flying the plane." And then the voice repeats, "last flight out cleared for takeoff."

The old plane begins to roll forward.

"Stop!" I holler. "Are you there? Air traffic control? I don't know how to fly!"

After a long pause, the voice says, "Yes you do. You've always known how to fly."

As the aircraft picks up speed, rattling down the runway, I belt myself into one of the seats and grab the steering wheel before me. As if on autopilot, the nose rises and we bump into the air, climbing higher and higher, the plane's windows filled with bright blue sky. And then higher still, yet I'm certain older aircraft like this were not meant to fly at so lofty an altitude—all the way to heaven—until, according to the altimeter, it maxes out at 333 kilometers an hour.

It is only when I can see the curvature of the earth below, on the edge of space, do I snap out of my wonderment and try to make sense of the instrument panel for taking control of the plane, of my life. But maybe it is too late, because the engines stall, causing an eerie silence, and the propellers flutter and sputter, and the nose changes trajectory from diagonally upward to diagonally downward, picking up speed, deeper into my own nightmare at 20,000 feet.

And I realize it must be all over.

No parachute.

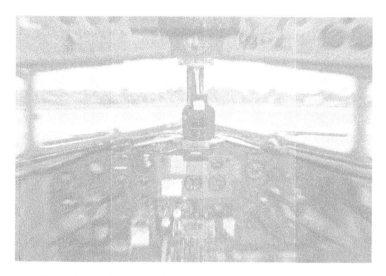

No other photograph.

No escape.

And I surrender to my fate.

And with surrender comes serenity, knowing I am one with the planet; that the universe is conscious, divine and I realize why all the world's traditional religions embody the same sacred truth: the spirit of God or Brahmin or Tao or Mother Nature is contained within ourselves, encompassing every molecule in every being, and that everything in the cosmos is quantum-ly entangled.

As the G-force intensifies with increasing speed I feel myself losing consciousness while at the same time feeling my spirit soar and I am filled with an overwhelming sense of serenity, of pure bliss.

24.

Slowly. Very slowly... I... open... my... eyes.

And awaken.

I'm looking up at a sky of obsidian snowflake—a moonless night featuring thousands of twinkling stars high above a dark restless ocean.

I glance around, somewhat dazed and confused, and realize I am in my old Jeep, in the parking area of Goleta State Park, near Santa Barbara Airport.

I straighten up, trying to pull myself together.

This thought reverberates my brain: *Did I fall asleep and never catch that last flight out?*

Finding myself here again—maybe awakening from a dream—is the only thing that makes any sense since I began my strange odyssey, what, three days ago?

I power my phone to check date and time and discover it is the same evening this began, maybe twenty minutes later, suggesting I have not gone anywhere at all.

A few bitchy texts are stacked up on my screen. Instead of allowing them to induce twinges of stress, I chuckle and let it pass through me.

I lower my window to take a deep breath, three deep breaths through my nose, filling my lungs with fresh salt air, not realizing until this precious moment the exquisiteness of oxygen.

Slowly, I gear into drive and roll onto Sandspit Road, not north to the airport, but east, heading home.

About fifteen seconds later, as I'm about to round into Ward Memorial Boulevard, rolling toward me from the other direction—headlights of shiny energy—is a Duesenberg convertible, late 1920s from the look of it.

I slow down to appreciate the immaculate beauty of this classic automobile, turquoise with silver metallic trimmings, and I catch a passing glimpse of the driver, a striking female

in a purple smoking jacket and mink scarf, waving at me and looking awfully like. . . *Louise Brooks?* She must be on her way to the airport, I muse, to catch the last flight out—albeit without me.

Picking up speed after veering onto I-101, the lightness I feel is contrasted by the weight of an object dangling from my neck.

Huh, what? No, couldn't be...

I tilt the rearview mirror and see, twinkling within its reflection, a silver Coptic Cross.